ENGAGED TO HER RAVENSDALE ENEMY

ENGAGED TO HER RAVENSDALE ENEMY

BY

MELANIE MILBURNE

First published in Great Britain 2016
By Mills & Boon, an imprint of HarperCollins*Publishers*
1 London Bridge Street, London, SE1 9GF

Large Print edition 2016

© 2016 Melanie Milburne

ISBN: 978-0-263-26221-6

Printed and bound in Great Britain
by CPI Antony Rowe, Chippenham, Wiltshire

To Monique Scott. You left an indelible mark on our family, enriching our lives in so many fabulous ways. You are the daughter I never had. You are the most amazing young woman, a gorgeous mother, and a wonderful friend. Love always. xxxx

CHAPTER ONE

IT WASN'T GIVING back the engagement ring Jasmine Connolly was most worried about. She had two more sitting in her jewellery box in her flat in Mayfair above her bridal-wear shop. It was the feeling of being rejected. *Again.* What was wrong with her? Why wasn't she good enough? She hadn't been good enough for her mother. Why did the people she cared about always leave her?

But that wasn't all that had her stomach knotting in panic. It was attending the winter wedding expo next weekend in the Cotswolds as a singleton. How could she front up *sans* fiancé? She might as well turn up at the plush hotel she'd booked months and months ago with 'loser' written on her forehead. She had so looked forward to that expo. After a lot of arm-twisting she had secured a slot in the fashion parade. It was her first catwalk show and it had the potential to lead to bigger and more important ones.

But it wasn't just about designing wedding gowns. She loved everything to do with weddings. The commitment to have someone love you for the rest of your life, not just while it was convenient or while it suited them. Love was supposed to be for ever. Every time she designed a gown she stitched her own hopes into it. What if she never got to wear one of her own gowns? What sort of cruel irony would that be?

She glanced at her empty ring finger where it was gripping the steering wheel. She wished she'd thought to shove on one of her spares just so she didn't have to explain to everyone that she was—to quote Myles—'taking a break'.

It didn't matter how he termed it, it all meant the same thing as far as Jaz was concerned. She was dumped. Jilted. Cast off. Single.

Forget about three times a bridesmaid, she thought sourly. What did it mean if you were three times a dumped fiancée?

It meant you sucked at relationships. Really sucked.

Jaz parked the car in her usual spot at Ravensdene, the family pile of the theatre-royalty family where she had grown up as the gardener's daughter and surrogate sister to Miranda Ravensdale and her older twin brothers, Julius and Jake.

Miranda had just got herself engaged. Damn. It.

Jaz was thrilled for her best mate. Of course she was. Miranda and Leandro Allegretti were perfect for each other. No one deserved a happy ending more than those two.

But why couldn't she have hers?

Jaz put her head down against the steering wheel and banged it three times. *Argh!*

There was a sound of a car growling as it

came up the long driveway. Jaz straightened and quickly got out of her car and watched as the Italian sports car ate up the gravel with its spinning tyres, spitting out what it didn't want in spraying arcs of flying stones. It felt like a fistful of those stones were clenched between her back molars as the car came to a dusty standstill next to hers.

Jacques, otherwise known as Jake, Ravensdale unfolded his tall, athletic frame from behind the wheel with animal grace. Jaz knew it was Jake and not his identical twin brother Julius because she had always been able to tell them apart. Not everyone could, but she could. She felt the difference in her body. Her body got all tingly and feverish, restless and antsy, whenever Jake was around. It was as if her body picked up a signal from his and it completely scrambled her motherboard.

His black hair was sexily tousled and windblown. Another reason to hate him, because she knew if she had just driven with the top down in that chilly October breeze her hair would have looked like a tangled fishing net. He was dressed casually because everything about Jake was casual, including his relationships—if you could call hook-ups and one-night stands relationships.

His dark-blue gaze was hidden behind designer aviator lenses but she could see a deep frown grooved into his forehead. At least it was a change from his stock-standard mocking smile. 'What the hell are you doing here?' he said.

Jaz felt another millimetre go down on her molars. 'Nice to see you too, Jake,' she said with a sugar-sweet smile. 'How's things? Had that personality transplant yet?'

He took off his sunglasses and continued to frown at her. 'You're supposed to be in London.'

Jaz gave him a wide-eyed, innocent look. 'Am I?'

'I checked with Miranda,' he said, clicking shut the driver's door with his foot. 'She said you were going to a party with Tim at his parents' house.'

'It's Myles,' she said. 'Tim was my…erm… other one.'

The corner of his mouth lifted. 'Number one or number two?'

It was extremely annoying how he made her ex-fiancés sound like bodily waste products, Jaz thought. Not that she didn't think of them that way too these days, but still. 'Number two,' she said. 'Lincoln was my first.'

Jake turned to pop open the boot of the car with his remote device. 'So where's lover-boy Myles?' he said. 'Is he planning on joining you?'

Jaz knew she shouldn't be looking at the way Jake's dark-blue denim jeans clung to his taut behind as he bent forward to get his overnight bag but what was a girl to do? He was built like an Olympic athlete. Lean and tanned with muscles in all the right places and in places where her exes didn't have them and never would. He was fantasy fodder. Ever since her hormones had been old enough to take notice, that was exactly what they had done. Which was damned inconvenient, since she absolutely, unreservedly loathed him. 'No…erm…he's staying in town to do some work,' she said. 'After the party, I mean.'

Jake turned back to look at her with a glinting smile. 'You've broken up.'

Jaz hated it that he didn't pose it as a question but as if it were a given. *Another Jasmine Connolly engagement bites the dust.* Not that she was going to admit it to him of all people. 'Don't be ridiculous,' she said. 'What on earth makes you think that? Just because I chose to spend the weekend down here while I work on Holly's dress instead of partying in town doesn't mean I'm—'

'Where's that flashy rock you've been brandishing about?'

Jaz used her left hand to flick her hair back over her shoulder in what she hoped was a casual manner. 'It's in London. I don't like wearing it when I'm working.' Which at least wasn't a complete lie. The ring was in London, safely in Myles' family jewellery vault. It miffed her Myles hadn't let her keep it. Not even for a few days till she got used to the idea of 'taking a break'. So what if it was a family heirloom? He had plenty of money. He could buy any number of rings. But no, he had to have it back, which meant she was walking around with a naked ring finger because she'd been too upset, angry and hurt to grab one of her other rings on her way out of the flat.

How galling if Jake were the first person to find out she had jinxed another relationship. How could she bear it? He wouldn't be sympathetic and consoling. He would roll about the floor laughing, saying, *I told you so.*

Jake hooked his finger through the loop on the collar of his Italian leather jacket and slung it over his shoulder. 'You'd better make yourself scarce if you're not in the mood for a party. I have guests arriving in an hour.'

Jaz's stomach dropped like a lift with snapped cables. 'Guests?'

His shoes crunched over the gravel as he strode towards the grand old Elizabethan mansion's entrance. 'Yep, the ones that eat and drink and don't sleep.'

She followed him into the house feeling like a teacup Chihuahua trying to keep up with an alpha wolf. 'What the hell? How many guests? Are they all female?'

He flashed her a white-toothed smile. 'You know me so well.'

Jaz could feel herself lighting up with lava-hot heat. Most of it burned in her cheeks at the thought of having to listen to him rocking on with a harem of his Hollywood wannabes. Unlike his identical twin brother Julius and his younger sister Miranda, who did everything they could to distance themselves from their parents' fame, Jake cashed in on it. Big-time. He was shameless in how he exploited it for all it was worth—which wasn't much, in Jaz's opinion. She had been the victim of his exploitative tactics when she'd been sixteen on the night of one of his parents' legendary New Year's Eve parties. He had led her on to believe he was serious about…

But she never thought about that night in his bedroom. *Never.*

'You can't have a party,' Jaz said as she followed him into the house. 'Mrs Eggleston's away. She's visiting her sister in Bath.'

'Which is why I've chosen this weekend,' he said. 'Don't worry. I've organised the catering.'

Jaz folded her arms and glowered at him. 'And

I bet I know what's on the menu.' *Him.* Being licked and ego-stroked by a bevy of bimbo airheads who drank champagne like it was water and ate nothing in case they put on an ounce. She only hoped they were all of age.

'You want to join us?'

Jaz jerked her chin back against her neck and made a scoffing noise. 'Are you out of your mind? I couldn't think of anything worse than watching a bunch of wannabe starlets get taken in by your particular version of charm. I'd rather chew razor blades.'

He shrugged one of his broad shoulders as if he didn't care either way. 'No skin off my nose.'

Jaz thought she would like to scratch every bit of skin off that arrogant nose. She hadn't been alone with him in years. There had always been other members of his family around whenever they'd come to Ravensdene. Why hadn't Eggles told her he would be here? Mrs Eggleston, the long-time housekeeper, knew how much Jaz hated Jake.

Everyone knew it. The feud between them had gone on for seven years. The air crackled with static electricity when they were in the same room even if there were crowds of other people around. The antagonism she felt towards Jake had grown exponentially every year. He had a habit of looking at her a certain way, as if he was thinking back to that night in his room when she had made the biggest fool of herself. His dark-blue eyes would take on a mocking gleam as if he could remember every inch of her body where it had been lying waiting for him in his bed in nothing but her underwear.

She gave a mental cringe. Yes, her underwear. What had she been thinking? Why had she fallen for it? Why hadn't she realised he'd been playing her for a fool? The humiliation he had subjected her to, the shame, the embarrassment of being hauled out of his bed in front of his… *Grrhh!* She would *not* think about it.

She. Would. Not.

Jaz's father wasn't even here to referee. He was away on a cruise of the Greek Islands with his new wife. Her father didn't belong to Jaz any more—not that he ever had. His work had always been more important than her. How could a garden, even one as big as the one at Ravensdene, be more important than his only child? But no, now he belonged to Angela.

Going back to London was out of the question. Jaz wasn't ready to announce the pause on her engagement. Not yet. Not until she knew for sure it was over. Not even to Miranda. Not while there was a slither of hope. All she had to do was make Myles see what he was missing out on. She was his soul mate. Of course she was. Everybody said so. Well, maybe not everybody, but she didn't need everyone's approval. Not even his parents' approval, which was a good thing, considering they didn't like her. But then, they were horrid toffee-nosed snobs and she didn't like them either.

Jaz did everything for Myles. She cooked, she cleaned, she organised his social calendar. She turned her timetable upside down and inside out so she could be available for him. She even had sex with him when she didn't feel like it. Which was more often than not, for some strange reason. Was that why Myles wanted a break? Because she wasn't sexually assertive enough? Not raunchy enough? She could do raunchy. She could wear dress-up costumes and play games. She would hate it but if it won him back she would do it. Other men found her attractive. Sure they did.

She was fighting off men all the time. She wasn't vain but she knew she had the package: the looks, the figure, the face and the hair. And she was whip-smart. She had her own bridal design company and she was not quite twenty-four.

Sure, she'd had a bit of help from Jake's parents, Richard and Elisabetta Ravensdale, in setting up. In fact, if it hadn't been for them, she wouldn't have had the brilliant education she'd had. They had stepped in when her mother had left her at Ravensdene on an access visit when she was eight and had never returned.

Not that it bothered Jaz that her mother hadn't come back for her. Not really. She was mightily relieved she hadn't had to go back to that cramped and mouldy, rat-infested flat in Brixton where the neighbours fought harder than the feral cats living near the garbage collection point. It was the principle of the thing that was the issue. Being left like a package on a doorstep wasn't exactly how one expected to be treated as a young child. But still, living at the Elizabethan mansion Ravensdene in Buckinghamshire had been much preferable. It was like being at a country spa resort with acres of verdant fields, dark, shady woods and a river meandering through the property like a silver ribbon.

This was home and the Ravensdales were family.

Well, apart from Jake, of course.

Jake tossed the bag on his bed and let out a filthy curse. What the hell was Jasmine Connolly doing here? He had made sure the place was empty for the weekend. He had a plan and Jasmine wasn't part of it. He did everything he could to avoid her. But when he couldn't he did everything he could to annoy her. He got a kick out of seeing her clench her teeth and flash those grey-blue eyes at him like tongues of flame. She was a pain in the backside but he wasn't going to let her dictate what he could and couldn't do. This was his family home, not hers. She might have benefited from being raised with his kid sister Miranda but she was still the gardener's daughter.

Jaz had been intent on marrying up since she'd been a kid. At sixteen she'd had her sights on him. *On him!* What a joke. He was ten years older than her; marriage hadn't been on his radar then and it wasn't on it now. It wasn't even in his vocabulary.

Jaz did nothing but think about marriage. Her whole life revolved around it. She was a good designer, he had to give her that, but it surely wasn't healthy to be so obsessed with the idea of marriage? Forty per cent of marriages ended in divorce—his parents' being a case in point. After his father's love-child scandal broke a month ago, it had looked like they were going to have a second one. The couple had remarried after their first divorce, and if another was on the way he only hoped it wouldn't be as acrimonious and publicly cringe-worthy as their last.

His phone beeped with an incoming message and he swore again when he checked his screen. Twenty-seven text messages and fourteen missed calls from Emma Madden. He had blocked her number but she must have borrowed someone else's phone. He knew if he checked his spam folder there would be just as many emails with photos of the girl's assets. Didn't that silly little teenager go to school? Where were her parents? Why weren't they monitoring her phone and online activity?

He was sick to the back teeth with teenaged girls with crushes. Jasmine had started it with her outrageous little stunt seven years ago. He'd had the last word on that. But this was a new era and Emma Madden wasn't the least put off by his efforts to shake her off. He'd tried being patient. He'd tried being polite. What was he supposed to do? The fifteen-year-old was like a leech, clinging on for all she was worth. He was being stalked. By a teenager! Sending him presents at work. Turning up at his favourite haunts, at the gym, at a business lunch, which was damned embarrassing. He'd had his work cut out trying to get his client to believe he wasn't doing a teenager. He might be a playboy but he had some standards and keeping away from underage girls was one of them.

Jake turned his phone to silent and tossed it next to his bag on the bed. He walked over to the window to look at the fields surrounding the country estate. Autumn was one of his favourite times at Ravensdene. The leaves on the deciduous trees in the garden were in their final stages of turning and the air was sharp and fresh with the promise of winter around the corner. As soon as his guests arrived he would light the fire in the sitting room, put on some music, pour the champagne, party on and post heaps of photos on social media so Emma Madden got the message.

Finally.

CHAPTER TWO

THE CARS STARTED arriving just as Jaz got comfortable in the smaller sitting room where she had set up her workstation. She had to hand-sew the French lace on Julius's fiancée Holly's dress, which would take hours. But she was happiest when she was working on one of her designs. She outsourced some of the basic cutting and sewing of fabric but when it came to the details she did it all by hand. It gave her designs that signature Jasmine Connolly touch. Every stitch or every crystal, pearl or bead she sewed on to a gown made her feel proud of what she had achieved. As a child she had sat on the floor in this very sitting room surrounded by butcher's paper or tissue wrap and Miranda as a willing, if not long-suffering, model. Jaz had dreamed of success. Success that would transport her far away from her status as the unwanted daughter of a barmaid who turned tricks to feed her drug and alcohol habit.

The sound of car doors slamming, giggling women and high heels tottering on gravel made Jaz's teeth grind together like tectonic plates. At this rate she was going to be down to her gums. But no way was she going back to town until the weekend was over. Jake could party all he liked. She was not being told what to do. Besides, she knew it would annoy him to have her here. He might have acted all cool and casual about it but she knew him well enough to know he would be spitting chips about it privately.

Jaz put down her sewing and carefully covered it with the satin wrapping sheet she had brought with her. This she had to see. What sort of women had he got to come? He had a thing for busty blondes. Such a cliché but that was Jake. He was shallow. He lived life in the fast lane and didn't stay in one place long enough to put down roots. He surrounded himself with showgirls and starlets who used him as much as he used them.

It was nauseating.

Jake was standing in the great hall surrounded by ten or so young women—all blonde—who were dressed in skimpy cocktail wear and vertiginous heels. Jaz leaned against the doorjamb with her arms folded, watching as each girl kissed him in greeting. One even ruffled his hair and another rubbed her breasts—which Jaz could tell were fake—against his upper arm.

He caught Jaz's eye and his mouth slanted in a mocking smile. 'Ah, here's the fun police. Ladies, this is the gardener's daughter, Jasmine.'

Jaz gave him an 'I'll get you for that later' look before she addressed the young women. 'Do your parents know where you all are?' she said.

Jake's brows shot together in a brooding scowl. 'Knock it off, Jasmine.'

Jaz smiled at him with saccharine sweetness. 'Just checking you haven't sneaked in a minor or two.'

Twin streaks of dull colour rode high along his aristocratic cheekbones and his mouth flattened until it was a bloodless line of white. A frisson of excitement coursed through her to have riled him enough to show a crack in his 'too cool for school' façade. Jaz was the only person who could do that to him. He sailed through life with that easy smile and that 'anything goes' attitude but pitted against her he rippled with latent anger. She wondered how far she could push him. Would he touch her? He hadn't come anywhere near her for seven years. When the family got together for Christmas or birthdays, or whatever, he never greeted her. He never hugged or kissed her on the cheek as he did to Miranda or his mother. He avoided Jaz like she was carrying some deadly disease, which was fine by her. She didn't want to touch him either.

But, instead of responding, Jake moved past her as if she was invisible and directed the women to the formal sitting room. 'In here, ladies,' he said. 'The party's about to begin.'

Jaz wanted to puke as the women followed him as though he were the Pied Piper. Couldn't they see how they were being used to feed his ego? He would ply them with expensive champagne or mix them exotic cocktails and tell them amusing anecdotes about his famous parents and their Hollywood and London theatre friends. Those he wouldn't bother sleeping with he would toss out by two or three in the morning. The one—or two or three, according to the tabloids—he slept with would be sent home once the deed was done. They would never get a follow-up call from him. It was a rare woman who got two nights with Jake Ravensdale. Jaz couldn't remember the last one.

The doorbell sounded behind her. She let out a weary sigh and turned to open it.

'I'll get that,' Jake said, striding back into the great hall from the sitting room.

Jaz stood to one side and curled her lip at him. 'Ten women not enough for you, Jake?'

He gave her a dismissive look and opened the door. But the smile of greeting dropped from his face as if he had been slapped. 'Emma…' His throat moved up and down. 'What? Why? How did you find me?' The words came spilling out in a way Jaz had never seen before. He looked agitated. *Seriously* agitated.

'I had to see you,' the girl said with big, lost waif, shimmering eyes and a trembling bottom lip. 'I just *had* to.'

And she was indeed a girl, Jaz noted. Not yet out of her teens. At that awkward age when one foot was in girlhood and the other in adulthood, a precarious position, and one when lots of silly mistakes that could last a lifetime could be made. Jaz knew it all too well. Hadn't she tried to straddle that great big divide, with devastating consequences?

'How'd you get here?' Jake's voice had switched from shocked to curt.

'I caught a cab.'

His brows locked together. 'All the way from London?'

'No,' Emma said. 'From the station in the village.'

Poor little kid, Jaz thought. She remembered looking at Jake exactly like that, as if he was some demigod and she'd been sent to this earth solely to worship him. It was cruel to watch knowing all the thoughts that were going through that young head. Teenage love could be so intense, so consuming and incredibly irrational. The poor kid was in the throes of a heady infatuation, travelling all this way in the hope of a little bit of attention from a man who clearly didn't want to give her the time of day. Jake was here partying with a bunch of women and Emma thought she could be one of them. What a little innocent.

Jaz couldn't stand by and watch history repeat itself. What if Emma was so upset she did something she would always regret, like *she* had done? There had to be a way to let the kid down in such a way that would ease the hurt of rejection. But brandishing a bunch of party girls in Emma's face was not the way to do it.

'Why don't you come in and I'll—?' Jaz began.

'Stay out of it, Jasmine,' Jake snapped. 'I'll deal with this.' He turned back to the girl. 'You have to leave. Now. I'll call you a cab but you have to go home. Understand?'

Emma's eyes watered some more. 'But I can't go home. My mother thinks I'm staying with a friend. I'll get in heaps of trouble. I'll be grounded for the rest of my life.'

'And so you damn well should be,' Jake growled.

'Maybe I could help,' Jaz said and held out her hand to the girl. 'I'm Jaz. I'm Jake's fiancée.'

There was a stunned silence.

Jake went statue-still beside Jaz. Emma looked at her with a blank stare. But then her cheeks pooled with crimson colour. 'Oh...I—I didn't realise,' she stammered. 'I thought Jake was still single otherwise I would never have—'

'It's fine, sweetie,' Jaz said. 'I totally understand and I'm not the least bit offended. We've been keeping our relationship a secret, haven't we, darling?' She gave Jake a bright smile while surreptitiously jabbing him in the ribs.

He opened and closed his mouth like a fish that had suddenly found itself flapping on the carpet instead of swimming safely in its fishbowl. But then he seemed to come back into himself and stretched his lips into one of his charming smiles. 'Yeah,' he said. 'That's right. A secret. I only just asked her a couple of minutes ago. That's why we're...er...celebrating.'

'Are you coming, Jakey?' A clearly tipsy blonde came tottering out into the hall carrying a bottle of champagne in one hand and a glass in the other.

Jaz took Emma by the arm and led her away to the kitchen, jerking her head towards Jake in a non-verbal signal to get control of his guest. 'That's one of the bridesmaids,' she said. 'Can't handle her drink. I'm seriously thinking of dumping her for someone else. I don't want her to spoil the wedding photos. Can you imagine?'

Emma chewed at her bottom lip. 'I guess it kind of makes sense...'

'What does?'

'You and Jake.'

Jaz pulled out a kitchen stool and patted it. 'Here,' she said. 'Have a seat while I make you a hot chocolate—or would you prefer tea or coffee?'

'Um...hot chocolate would be lovely.'

Jaz got the feeling Emma had been about to

ask for coffee in order to appear more sophisticated. It reminded her of all the times when she'd drunk vile-tasting cocktails in order to fit in. She made the frothiest hot chocolate she could and handed it to the young girl. 'Here you go.'

Emma cupped her hands around the mug like a child. 'Are you sure you're not angry at me turning up like this? I had no idea Jake was serious about anyone. There's been nothing in the press or anything.'

'No, of course not,' Jaz said. 'You weren't to know.' *I didn't know myself until five minutes ago.* 'We haven't officially announced it yet. We wanted to have some time to ourselves before the media circus begins.' And it would once the news got out. Whoopee doo! If this didn't get Myles' attention, nothing would.

'You're the gardener's daughter,' Emma said. 'I read about you in one of the magazines at the hairdresser's. There was an article about

Jake's father's love-child Katherine Winwood and there were pictures of you. You've known Jake all your life.'

'Yes, since I was eight,' Jaz said. 'I've been in love with him since I was sixteen.' *It didn't hurt to tell her one more little white lie, did it? It was all in a good cause.* 'How old are you?'

'Fifteen and a half,' Emma said.

'Tough age.'

Emma's big brown eyes lowered to study the contents of her mug. 'I met Jake at a function a couple of months ago,' she said. 'It was at my stepfather's restaurant. He sometimes lets me work for him as a waitress. Jake was the only person who was nice to me that night. He even gave me a tip.'

'Understandable you'd fancy yourself in love with him,' Jaz said. 'He breaks hearts just by breathing.'

Emma's mouth lifted at the corners in a vestige of a smile. 'I should hate you but I don't.

You're too nice. Kind of natural and normal, you know? But then, I guess I would hate you if I didn't think you were perfect for him.'

Jaz smiled over clenched teeth. 'How about we give your mum a call and let her know where you are? Then I'll drive you to the station and wait with you until you get on the train, okay? Have you got a mobile?'

Silly question. What teenager didn't? It was probably a better model than hers.

When Jaz got back from sending Emma on her way home, Jake was in the main sitting room clearing away the detritus of his short-lived party. Apparently he had sent his guests on their merry way as well. 'Need some help with that?' she said.

He sent her a black look. 'I think you've done more than enough for one night.'

'I thought it was a stroke of genius, actually,' Jaz said, calmly inspecting her nails.

'Engaged?' he said. '*Us?* Don't make me laugh.'

He didn't look anywhere near laughing, Jaz thought. His jaw was locked like a stiff hinge. His mouth was flat. His eyes were blazing with fury. 'What else was I supposed to do?' she said. 'That poor kid was so love-struck nothing short of an engagement would've convinced her to leave.'

'I had it under control,' he said through tight lips.

Jaz rolled her eyes. 'How? By having a big bimbo bash? Like that was ever going to work. You're going about this all wrong, Jake—or should I call you Jakey?'

His eyes flashed another round of sparks at her. 'That silly little kid has been stalking me for weeks. She gate-crashed an important business lunch last week. I lost a valuable client because of her.'

'She's young and fancies herself in love,' Jaz

said. 'You were probably the first man to ever speak to her as if she was a real person instead of a geeky kid. But throwing a wild party with heaps of women isn't going to convince her you're not interested in her. The only way was to convince her you're off the market. Permanently.'

He snatched up a half-empty bottle of champagne and stabbed the neck of it in her direction. 'You're the last woman on this planet I would ever ask to marry me.'

Jaz smiled. 'I know. Isn't it ironic?'

His jaw audibly ground together. 'What's your fiancé going to say about this?'

Here's the payoff. She would have to tell Jake about the break-up. But it would be worth it if it achieved the desired end. 'Myles and I are having a little break for a month,' she said.

'You conniving little cow,' he said. 'You're using me to make him jealous.'

'We're using each other,' Jaz corrected. 'It's a

win-win. We'll only have to pretend for a week or two. Once the hue and cry is over we can go back to being frenemies.'

His frown was so deep it closed the gap between his eyes. 'You're thinking of making an... *an announcement*?'

Jaz held up her phone. 'Already done. Twitter is running hot with it. Any minute now I expect your family to start calling.' As if on cue, both of their phones starting ringing.

'Don't answer that.' He quickly muted his phone. 'We need to think this through. We need a plan.'

Jaz switched her phone to silent but not before she saw Myles' number come up. Good. All going swimmingly so far. 'We can let your family in on the secret if you think they'll play ball.'

'It's too risky.' Jake scraped a hand through his hair. 'If anyone lets slip we're not the real deal, it could blow up in our faces. You know what the press are like. Do you think Emma bought it? Really?'

'Yes, but she'll know something's up if you don't follow through.'

He frowned again. 'Follow through how? You're not expecting me to marry you, are you?'

Jaz gave him a look that would have withered a plastic flower. 'I'm marrying Myles, remember?'

'If he takes you back after this.'

She heightened her chin. 'He will.'

One side of his mouth lifted in a cynical arc. 'What's Miranda going to say? You think she'll accept you're in love with me?'

Miranda was going to be a hard sell, but Jaz knew she didn't like Myles, so perhaps it would work. For a time. 'I don't like lying to Miranda, but she's never been…'

'You should've thought of that when you cooked up this stupid farce,' Jake said. 'No. We'll run with it.'

'What did you tell your party girls?' Jaz said. 'I hope I didn't make things too awkward for you.' Ha ha. She *loved* making things awkward for him. The more awkward, the better. What a hoot it was to see him squirm under the shackles of a commitment.

'I'm not in the habit of explaining myself to anyone,' he said. 'But no doubt they'll hear the news like everyone else.'

Jaz glanced at her bare ring finger. Who would take their engagement seriously unless she had evidence? 'I haven't got a ring.'

His dark eyes gleamed with malice. 'No spares hanging around at home?'

She sent him a beady look. 'Do you really want me to wear some other man's ring?'

His mouth flattened again. 'Right. I'll get you a ring.'

'No fake diamonds,' she said. 'I want the real thing. The sort of clients I attract can tell the difference, you know.'

'This is what this is all about, isn't it?' he said. 'You don't want your clients to think you can't hold a man long enough to get him to marry you.'

Jaz could feel her anger building like a catastrophic storm inside her. This wasn't about what her clients thought. It was about what *she* felt. No one in their right mind wanted to be rejected. Abandoned. To be told they weren't loved in the way she desperately dreamed of being loved. Not after she had invested so much in her relationship with Myles.

What did Jake know of investing in a relationship? He moved from one woman to the next without a thought of staying long enough to get to know someone beyond what they liked to do in bed. Only Jake could make her this angry— angry enough to throw something. It infuriated her that he alone could reduce her to such a state. 'I can hold a man,' she said. 'I can hold him just fine. Myles has cold feet, that's all. It's perfectly normal for the groom to get a little stressed before the big day.'

'If he loved you he wouldn't ask for a break,' Jake said. 'He wouldn't risk you finding someone else.'

That thought had occurred to Jaz but she didn't want to think about it. She was good at not thinking about things she didn't want to think about. 'Listen to you,' she said with a scornful snort. 'Jake Ravensdale, playboy extraordinaire, talking like a world expert on love.'

'Where did you take Emma?'

'I put her on the train once I'd talked to her mother and made sure everything was cool,' Jaz said. 'I didn't want her to get into trouble or do anything she might regret.' *Like I did.* She pushed the thought aside. She wouldn't think about the rest of that night after she had left Jake's bedroom.

Jake picked up a glass, filled it with champagne and knocked it back in one gulp. He

shook his head like a dog coming out of water
and then poured another glass. With his features
cast in such serious lines, he looked more like
his twin Julius than ever.

'We need a photo,' Jaz said. 'Hand me a glass.'

He looked at her as if she had just asked him
to poke a knitting needle in his eye. 'A photo?'
he said. 'What for?'

She helped herself to a glass of champagne
and came to stand beside him but he backed
away as if she was carrying dynamite. Or knitting needles. 'Get away from me,' he said.

'We have to do this, Jake,' she said. 'Who's
going to believe it if we don't do an engagement
photo?'

'You don't have a ring,' he said. 'Yet.' The
way he said 'yet' made it sound as though he
considered the task on the same level as having
root canal therapy.

'Doesn't matter,' Jaz said. 'Just a shot with

us with a glass of champers and grinning like Cheshire cats will be enough.'

'You're a sadist,' he said, shooting her a hooded look as she came to stand beside him with her camera phone poised. 'You know that, don't you? A totally sick sadist.'

It was impossible for Jaz not to notice how hard and warm his arm was against hers as she leaned in to get the shot. Impossible not to think of those strongly muscled arms gathering her even closer. Was he as aware of her as she was of him? Was that why he was standing so still? He hadn't been this close to her in years. When family photographs had been taken— even though strictly speaking she wasn't family—she had always been up the other end of the shot close to Miranda or one of Jake's parents. She had never stood right next to Jake. Not so close she could practically feel the blood pumping through his veins. She checked the photo and groaned. 'Oh, come on,' she said. 'Surely you can do better than that. You look like some-one's got a broomstick up your—'

'Okay, we'll try again.' He put an arm around her shoulders and leaned his head against hers. She could feel the strands of his tousled hair tickling her skin. Her senses were going hay-wire when his stubbly jaw grazed her face. He smelt amazing—lime and lemongrass with a hint of ginger or some other spice. 'Go on,' he said. 'Take the goddamn shot.'

'Oh…right,' Jaz said and clicked the button. She checked the photo but this time it looked like she was the one being tortured. Plus it was blurred. 'Not my best angle.' She deleted it and held up the phone. 'One more take. Say cheese.'

'That's enough,' he said, stepping away from her once she'd taken the shot. 'You have to promise me you'll delete that when this is all over, okay?'

Jaz criss-crossed her chest with her hand. 'Cross my heart and hope to die.'

He grunted as if her demise was something he was dearly praying for.

She sent the tweet and then quickly sent a text to Miranda:

I know you never liked Myles. You approve of fiancé # 4?

Miranda's text came back within seconds.

OMG! Definitely!!! Congrats. Always knew you were hot for each other. J Will call later xxxxx

'Who are you texting?' Jake asked.

'Miranda,' Jaz said, putting her phone down. 'She's thrilled for us. We'll finally be sisters. Yay.'

He muttered a curse and prowled around the room like a shark in a fishbowl. 'Julius is never going to fall for this. Not for a moment.'

'He'll have to if you want Emma to go away,' Jaz said. 'If you don't play along I'll tell her the truth.'

He threw her a filthy look. 'You're enjoying this, aren't you?'

She smiled a victor's smile. 'What's that saying about revenge is a dish best eaten cold?'

He glowered at her. 'Isn't it a little childish to be harking on about that night all these years later? I did you a favour back then. I could've done you that night but how would that have worked out? Ever thought about that? No. You want to paint me as the big, bad guy who made you feel a little embarrassed about that schoolgirl crush. But, believe me, I could have done a whole lot worse.'

Jaz stepped out of his way as he stormed past her to leave the room. *You did do a whole lot worse*, she wanted to throw after him. But instead she clamped her lips together and turned back to look at the discarded bottles and glasses.

Typical. Jake had a habit of leaving his mess for other people to clean up.

CHAPTER THREE

JAKE WAS SO mad he could see red spots in front
of his eyes. Or maybe he was having a brain an-
eurysm from anger build-up. Seven years of it.
He paced the floor of his room, raking his hair,
grinding his teeth, swearing like a Brooklyn
rapper at what Jasmine had done to him. Engaged! What a freaking farce. No one would
believe it. Not him. Not the playboy prince of
the pick-ups.

His stomach turned at the thought. Committed. Tied down. Trapped. He was the last person who would ever tie himself down to one
woman and certainly not someone like Jasmine
Connolly. She was a manipulative little witch.
She was using him. Using him to lure back her
third fiancé. Who on earth got engaged three

times? Someone who was obsessed with getting married, that was who. Jasmine didn't seem to care who she got engaged to as long as they had money and status.

But through the red mist of anger he could see her solution had some merit. Emma Madden had taken the news of their 'engagement' rather well. He had been poleaxed to see that kid standing on the doorstep. He could count on half a hand how many times he'd been caught off guard but seeing that kid there was right up there. If anyone had seen her—anyone being the press, that was—he would have been toast. He didn't want to be cruel to the girl but how else could he get rid of her? Jasmine's solution seemed to have worked. So far. But how long would he have to stay 'engaged'?

Then there was his family to deal with. He could probably pull off the lie with his parents and Miranda but not his twin. Julius knew him too well. Julius knew how much he hated the thought of being confined in a relationship. Jake was more like his father in that way. His father wasn't good at marriage. Richard and Elisabetta fought as passionately as they made up. It was a war zone one minute and a love fest the next. As a child Jake had found it deeply unsettling—not that he'd ever showed it. His role in the family was the court jester. It was his way of coping with the turbulent emotions that flew around like missiles. He'd never known what he was coming home to.

Then eventually it had happened. The divorce had been bitter and public and the intrusion of the press terrifying to a child of eight. He and Julius had been packed off to boarding school but, while Julius had relished the routine, structure and discipline, Jake had not. Julius had excelled academically while Jake had scraped through, not because he wasn't intellectually capable but because in an immature and mostly subconscious way he hadn't wanted his parents to think their divorce had had a positive effect on him.

But he had more than made up for it in his business analysis company. He was successful and wealthy and had the sort of life most people envied. The fly-in, fly-out nature of his work suited his personality. He didn't hang around long. He just got in there, sorted out the problems and left. Which was how he liked to conduct his relationships.

Being tied to Jasmine, even if it was only a game of charades, was nothing less than torture. He had spent the last seven years avoiding her. Distancing himself from all physical contact. He had even failed to show up for some family functions in an effort to avoid the tension of being in the same room as her. He'd had plenty of lectures from Julius and Miranda about fixing things with Jasmine but why should *he* apologise? He hadn't done anything wrong. He had done the opposite. He had solved the problem, not made it worse. It was her that was still in a snit over something she should have got over years ago.

She had been a cute little kid but once she'd hit her teens she'd changed into a flirty little vamp. It had driven him nuts. She had followed him around like a loyal puppy, trying to sneak time with him, touching him 'by accident' and batting those impossibly long eyelashes at him. He had gone along with it for a while, flirting back in a playful manner, but in the end that had backfired, as she'd seemed to think he was serious about her. He wasn't serious about anyone. But on the night of his parents New Year's Eve party, when she'd been sixteen and he twenty-six, he had drawn the line. He'd activated a plan to give her the message loud and clear: He was a player, not the soppy, romantic happy-ever-after beau she imagined him to be.

That night she had dressed in a revealing outfit that was far too old for her and had worn make-

up far too heavy. To Jake she had looked like
a kid who had rummaged around in her mother's wardrobe. In the dark. He had gone along
with her flirtation all evening, agreeing to meet
with her in his room just after midnight. But instead of turning up alone as she'd expected he'd
brought a couple of girls with him, intending to
shock Jasmine into thinking he was expecting
an orgy. It had certainly done the trick. She had
left him alone ever since. He couldn't remember
the last time she had spoken to him other than
to make some cutting remark and the only time
she looked at him was to spear him with a death-
adder glare. Which had suited him just fine.

Until now.

Now he had to work out a way of hanging
around with her without wanting to… Well, he
didn't want to admit to what he wanted to do
with her. But he was only human and a full-
blooded male, after all. She was the stuff of male
fantasies. He would never admit it to anyone but

over the years he'd enjoyed a few fantasies of her in his morning shower. She was sultry and sulky, yet she had a razor-sharp wit and intelligence to match. She had done well for herself, building her business up from scratch, although he thought she was heading for a burnout by trying to do everything herself. Not that she would ever ask his advice. She was too proud. She would rather go bankrupt than admit she might have made a mistake.

Jake dragged a hand down his face. This was going to be the longest week or two of his life. What did Jasmine expect of him? How far did she want this act to go? She surely wouldn't want to sleep with him if she was still hankering after her ex? Not that she showed any sign of being attracted to him, although she did have a habit of looking at his mouth now and again. But everyone knew how much she hated him. Not that a bit of hate got in the way of good sex.

Sheesh. He had to stop thinking about sex and

Jasmine in the same sentence. He had never seen her as a sister, even though she had been brought up as one at Ravensdene. Or at least not since she'd hit her teens. She'd grown from being a gangly, awkward teenager into an unusual but no less stunning beauty. Her features were not what one could describe as classically beautiful, but there was some indefinable element to the prominence of her brows and the ice-blue and storm-grey of her eyes that made her unforgettable. She had a model-slim figure and lustrous, wavy honey-brown hair that fell midway down her back. Her skin was creamy and smooth and looked fabulous with or without make-up, although she used make-up superbly these days.

Her mouth… How could he describe it? It was perfect. Simply perfect. He had never seen a more beautiful mouth. The lower lip was full and shapely, the top one a perfect arc above it. The vermillion borders of her lips were so neatly aligned it was as if a master had drawn them. She had a way of slightly elevating her chin, giving her a haughty air that belied her humble beginnings. Her nose, too, had the look of an aristocrat about it with its ski-slope contour. When she smiled—which she rarely did when he was around—it lit up the room. He had seen grown men buckle at the knees at that smile.

Jake's phone vibrated where he'd left it on the bedside table. He glanced at the screen and saw it was Julius. His twin had called six times now. *Better get it over with*, he thought, and answered.

'Is this some kind of prank?' Julius said without preamble.

'No, it's—'

'Jaz and you?' Julius cut him off. 'Come on, man. You hate her guts. You can't stand being in the same room as her. What happened?'

'It was time to bury the hatchet,' Jake said.

'You think I came down in the last shower?'

Julius said. 'I know wedding fever has hit with Holly and me, and now Miranda and Leandro, but you and Jaz? I don't buy it for a New York picosecond. What's she got on you? Is she holding a AK-47 to your head?'

Jake let out a rough-edged sigh. He could lie to anyone else but not his identical twin. All that time in the womb had given them a connection beyond what normal siblings felt. They even felt each other's pain. When Julius had had his appendix out when he was fifteen Jake had felt like someone was ripping his guts out. 'I've been having a little problem with a girl,' he said. 'A teenager.'

'I'm not sure I want to hear this.'

'It's not what you think,' Jake said and explained the situation before adding, 'Jasmine intercepted Emma at the door and told her we were engaged.'

'How did this girl Emma take it?'

'Surprisingly well,' Jake said.

'What about Jaz's fiancé?'

'I have no idea,' Jake said. 'He's either relieved she's off his hands or he's going to turn up at my place and shoot out my kneecaps.'

'Always a possibility.'

'Don't remind me.'

There was a beat of silence.

'You're not going to sleep with her, are you?' Julius said.

'God, no,' Jake said. 'I wouldn't touch her with a barge pole.'

'Yes, well, I suggest you keep your barge pole zipped in your pants,' Julius said dryly. 'What actually happened with you guys that night at the party? I know she came to your room but you've never said what went on other than you didn't touch her.'

'I didn't do anything except send her on her way,' Jake said. 'You know what she was like, always following me about, giving me sheep's eyes. I taught her a lesson by offering her a four-some but she declined.'

'A novel approach.'

'It worked.'

'Maybe, but don't you think her anger is a little out of proportion?' Julius said.

'That's just Jasmine,' Jake said. 'She's always had a rotten temper.'

'I don't know... I sometimes wonder if something else happened that night.'

'Like what?'

'She'd been drinking and was obviously upset after leaving your room,' Julius said. 'Not a good combination in a teenage girl.'

Jake hung up a short time later once they'd switched topics but he couldn't get rid of the seed of unease Julius had planted in his mind. Had something happened that night after Jasmine had left his room? Was that why she had been so protective of young Emma, making sure she got home safely with an adult at the other end to meet her? The rest of that night was a bit of blur for him. Most of his parents' parties ended up that way. Even some of his parties were a little full-on too. There was always a lot of alcohol, loud music blaring and people coming and going. He had been feeling too pleased with himself for solving the Jasmine problem to give much thought to where she'd gone after leaving his room. At twenty-six what he had done had seemed the perfect solution. The only solution.

Now, at thirty-three, he wasn't quite so sure.

Jaz was making herself a nightcap in the kitchen when Jake strolled in. 'Finding it hard to sleep without a playgirl bunny or three in your bed to keep you warm?'

'What happened after you left my room that night?'

Jaz lowered her gaze to her chocolate drink rather than meet his piercing blue eyes. The chocolate swirled as she stirred it with the tea-spoon, creating a whirlpool not unlike the one she could feel in the pit of her stomach. She never thought about that night. That night had happened to another person. It had happened to a foolish, gauche kid who'd had too much to drink and had been too emotionally unstable to know what she was doing or what she was getting into.

'Jasmine. Answer me.'

Jaz lifted her gaze to his and frowned. 'Why do you always call me Jasmine instead of Jaz? You're the only one in your family who insists on doing that. Why?'

'It's your name.'

'So? Yours is Jacques but you don't like being called that,' Jaz pointed out. 'Maybe I'll start to.'

'Julius knows.'

Her heart gave a little stumble. 'Knows what?'

'About us,' he said. 'About this not being real.'

Jaz took a moment to get her head sorted.

She'd thought he meant Julius knew about *that night*… But how could he? He would have said something if he did. He was the sort of man who would have got her to press charges. He wouldn't have stood by and let someone get away with it.

'Oh…right; well, I guess he's your twin and all.'

'He won't tell anyone apart from Holly.'

'Good,' Jaz said. 'The less people who know, the better.'

Jake pulled out a kitchen stool and sat opposite her at the island bench. 'You want to make me one of those?'

She lifted her chin. 'Make it yourself.'

A slow smile came to his mouth. 'I guess I'd better in case you put cyanide in it.'

Jaz forced her gaze away from the tempting curve of his mouth. It wasn't fair that one man had so much darn sex appeal. It came off him in waves. She felt it brush against her skin, making her body tingle at the thought of him touching her for real. Ever since his arm had brushed against hers, ever since he'd slung his arm around her shoulders and leaned in against her, she had longed for him to do it again. It was like every nerve under her skin was sitting bolt upright and wide awake, waiting with bated breath for him to touch her again.

She was aware of him in other parts of her body. The secret parts. Her breasts and inner core tingled from the moment he'd stepped into the same room. It was like he could turn a switch in her body simply by being present. She watched covertly as he moved about the kitchen, fetching a cup and the tin of chocolate powder and stirring it into the milk before he turned to put it in the microwave.

She couldn't tear her eyes away from his back and shoulders. He was wearing a cotton T-shirt that showcased every sculpted muscle on his frame. How would it feel to slide her hands down his tautly muscled back? To slip one of her hands past the waistband of his jeans and cup his trim buttocks, or what was on the other side of his testosterone-rich groin?

Jaz gave herself a mental shake. She was on a mission to win back Myles. Getting involved with Jake was out of the question. Not that he would ever want *her*. He loathed her just as much as she loathed him. But men could separate their emotions from sex. She of all people knew that. Maybe he would want to make the most of their situation—a little fling to pass the time until he could get back to his simpering starlets and Hollywood hopefuls. Her mind started to drift… What would it feel like to have Jake make love to her? To have his hands stroke every inch of her flesh, to have his mouth plunder hers?

Jake turned from the microwave. 'Is something wrong?'

Jaz blinked to reset her vision. 'That was weird. I thought I saw you actually lift a finger in the kitchen. I must be hallucinating.'

He laughed and pulled out one of the stools opposite hers at the kitchen bench. 'I can find my way around a kitchen when I need to.'

Jaz's top lip lifted in a cynical arc. 'Like when no slavishly devoted woman is there to cater to your every whim?'

His eyes held hers in a penetrating lock. She felt the power of it go through her like a current of electricity. 'How much did you have to drink that night?' he asked.

She pushed her untouched chocolate away and slipped off the stool. 'Clean up your mess when you're done in here. Eggles won't be back till Sunday night.'

Jaz almost got to the door, but then Jake's hand came out of nowhere and turned her to face him. His warm, strong fingers curling around her arm sent a shockwave through her body, making her feel as if someone inside her stomach had shuffled a deck of cards. Quickly. Vegas-quick. She moistened her lips with her tongue as she brought her gaze to his dark-blue one. His ink-black lashes were at half-mast, giving him a sexily hooded look. She looked at his mouth and felt that shuffle in her heart valves this time. She could look at his twin's mouth any time without this crazy reaction. What was it about Jake's mouth that turned her into a quivering mess of female hormones? Was it because, try as she might, she couldn't stop thinking about how it would feel pressed to hers? 'I don't remember giving you permission to touch me,' she said.

Instead of releasing her he slid his fingers down to the bones of her wrist and encircled it like a pair of gentle handcuffs. 'Talk to me,' he said in a deep, gravel-rough voice that made the entire length of her spine soften like candle wax in a steam room.

Jaz tested his hold but all it did was take him with her to the doorframe, which was just an inch or so behind her. She pressed her back against it for stability because right then her legs weren't doing such a great job of holding her upright. He was now so close she could see the individual pinpricks of stubble along his jaw and around his nose and mouth. She could feel their breath intermingling. His muscle-packed thighs were within a hair's breadth of hers, his booted feet toe-to-toe with her bare ones. 'Wh-what are you doing?' she said in a voice she barely recognised as her own.

His eyes went to her mouth, lingering there for endless, heart-stopping seconds. 'Ever wondered what would happen if we kissed?'

Like just about every day for the last seven years. 'You'd get your face slapped, that's what.'

A smile hitched up one side of his mouth. 'Yeah, that's what I thought.'

Jaz felt like her heart rate was trying to get into the *Guinness Book of Records*. She could smell those lime and lemongrass notes of his aftershave and something else that was one part musk and three parts male. 'But you're not going to do it, right?'

He moved around her mouth like a metal detector just above the ground where something valuable was hidden. He didn't touch down but he might as well have because she felt the tingling in her lips as if he was transmitting raw sexual energy from his body to hers. 'You think about it, don't you? About us getting down to business.'

Oh, dear God in heaven, where is my willpower? Jaz thought as her senses went haywire. She had never wanted to be kissed more in her life than right then. She had never wanted to feel a man's arms go around her and pull her into his hard body. Desire moved through her like a prowling, hungry beast looking for satiation. She felt it in her blood, the tick of arousal. She felt it in her breasts, the prickly sensation of them shifting against the lace of her bra as if they couldn't wait for him to get his hands or mouth on them. She felt it in her core, the pulse and contraction of her inner muscles in anticipatory excitement. 'No, I don't. I never think about it.'

He gave a soft chuckle as he stepped back from her. 'No, nor do I.'

Jaz stood in numb silence as he went back to the island bench to pick up his hot chocolate. She watched as he lifted the mug to his lips and took a sip. He put the mug down and cocked a brow at her. 'Something wrong?'

She pushed herself away from the doorframe, tucking her hair back over one shoulder with a hand that wasn't as steady as she would have liked. 'We haven't discussed the rules about our engagement.'

'Rules?'

Jaz gave him a look. 'Yes, rules. Not your favourite word, is it?'

His eyes glinted. 'Far as I'm concerned, they're only there to be broken.'

She steeled her spine. 'Not this time.'

'Is that a dare?'

Jaz could feel every cell in her body being pulled and tugged by the animal attraction he evoked in her. She couldn't understand why someone she hated so much could have such a monumental effect on her. She wanted to throw herself at him, tear at his clothes and crawl all over his body. She wanted to lock her mouth on his and tangle her tongue with his in an erotic salsa. She wanted him *inside* her body. She could feel the hollow vault of her womanhood pulsating with need. She could even feel the dew of her intimate moisture gathering. She wanted him like a drug she knew she shouldn't have. He was contraband. Dangerous. 'Is the thought of being celibate for a week or two really that difficult for you?'

He gave a lip shrug. 'Never done it before, so I wouldn't know.'

Jaz mentally rolled her eyes. 'Do you have

shares in a condom manufacturer or something?'

His dark eyes gleamed with amusement. 'Now there's an idea.'

She picked up her mug of chocolate, not to drink, but to give her hands something to do in case they took it upon themselves to touch him. 'I find your shallow approach to relationships deeply offensive. It's like you only see women as objects you can use to satisfy a bodily need. You don't see them as real people who have feelings.'

'I have the greatest respect for women. That's why I'm always honest with them about what I want from them.'

Jaz eyeballed him. 'I think it's because you're scared of commitment. You can't handle the thought of someone leaving you so you don't let yourself bond with them in the first place.'

He gave a mocking laugh. 'You got a printout of that psychology degree you bought online?'

'That's another thing you do,' Jaz said. 'You joke your way through life because being serious about stuff terrifies you.'

His mouth was smiling but his eyes were not. They had become as hard as flint. 'Ever wondered why your three fiancés have dumped you before you could march them up the aisle?'

Jaz ground her teeth together until her jaw ached. 'Myles hasn't dumped me. We're on a break. It's not the same as being…breaking up.'

'You're a ballbreaker. You don't want a man. You want a puppet. Someone you can wind around your little finger to do what you want when you want. No man worth his testosterone will stand for that.'

Jaz could feel her anger straining at the leash of her control like a feral dog tied up with a piece of cotton. Her fingers around the mug of chocolate twitched. How she would love to spray it over Jake's arrogant face. 'You enjoy humiliating me, don't you? It gives you such a big, fat hard-on, doesn't it?'

His jaw worked as if her words had hit a raw nerve. 'While we're playing Ten Things I Hate About You, here's another one for my list. You need to get over yourself. You've held onto this ridiculous grudge for far too long.'

Jaz saw the hot chocolate fly through the air before she fully registered she'd thrown it. It splashed over the front of his T-shirt like brown paint thrown at a wall.

Jake barely moved a muscle. He was as still as a statue on a plinth. Too still.

The silence was breathing, heaving with menace.

But then he calmly reached over the back of his head, hauled the T-shirt off, bunched it up into a rough ball and handed it to her. 'Wash it.'

Jaz swallowed as she looked at the T-shirt. She had lost control. A thing she had sworn she would never do. Crazy people like her mother lost control. They shouted and screamed and threw things. Not her. She never let anyone do that to her. A tight knot of self-disgust began to choke her. Tears welled up behind her eyes, escaping from a place she had thought she had locked and bolted for good. Tears she hadn't cried since that night when she had finally made it back to her bedroom with shame clinging to her like filth. No amount of showering had removed it. If she thought about that night she would feel it clogging every pore of her skin like engine grease. She took the T-shirt from him with an unsteady hand. 'I'm sorry...'

'Forget about it.'

I only wish I could, Jaz thought. But when she finally worked up the courage to look up he had already turned on his heel and gone.

CHAPTER FOUR

JAKE WAS VAINLY trying to sleep when he heard the sound of the plumbing going in the other wing of the house where Jasmine's room was situated next to Miranda's. He lay there for a while, listening as the pipes pumped water. Had Jasmine left on a tap? He glanced at the bedside clock. It was late to be having a shower, although he had to admit for him a cold one wouldn't have gone astray. He rarely lost his temper. He preferred to laugh his way out of trouble but something about Jasmine's mood had got to him tonight. He was sick of dragging their history around like a dead carcass. It was time to put it behind them. He didn't want Julius and Holly's or Miranda and Leandro's wedding ruined by a ridiculous feud that had gone on way too long.

He shoved off the bed covers and reached for a bathrobe. He seemed to remember Jasmine had a tendency for long showers but he still thought he'd better check to make sure nothing was amiss. He made his way to the bathroom closest to her room and rapped his knuckles on the door. 'You okay in there?' he said. No answer. He tapped again, louder this time, and called out but the water continued. He tried the door but it was locked. He frowned. Why did she think she had to lock the door? They were alone in the house. Didn't she trust him? The thought sat uncomfortably on him. He might be casual about sex but not *that* casual. He always ensured he had consent first.

Not that he was going to sleep with Jasmine. That would be crazy. Crazy but tempting. Way too tempting, if he was honest with himself. He had spent many an erotic daydream with her body pinned under his or over his, or with her mouth on him, sucking him until he blew like a bomb. She had that effect on men. She didn't do it on purpose; her natural sensuality made men fall over like ninepins. Her beauty, her regal manner, her haughty 'I'm too good for the likes of you' air made men go weak at the knees, himself included. Just thinking about her naked body under that spray of water in the shower was enough to make him rock-hard.

He waited outside her door until the water finally stopped. 'Jasmine?'

It was a while before she opened the door. She was wearing a bathrobe and her hair was wrapped turban-like with a towel. Her skin was rosy from the hot water and completely make-up free, giving her a youthful appearance that took him back a decade. 'What?' She frowned at him irritably. 'Is something wrong with your bathroom?'

He frowned when he saw her red-rimmed eyes and pink nose. 'Have you been crying?'

Her hand clutching the front of her bathrobe clenched a little tighter but her tone was full of derision. 'Why would I be crying? Oh, yes, I remember now. My fiancé wanted a month's break. Pardon me for being a little upset.'

Jake felt a stab of remorse for not having factored in her feelings. He had such an easy come, easy go attitude to his relationships he sometimes forgot other people invested much more emotionally. But did she really love the guy or was she in love with the idea of love and marriage? Three engagements in three years. That must be some sort of record, surely? Had she been in love each time? 'You want to talk about it?'

Her eyes narrowed in scorn. 'What—with *you*?'

'Why not?'

She pushed past him and he got a whiff of

honeysuckle body wash. 'I'm going to bed. Good night.'

'Jasmine, wait,' Jake said, capturing her arm on the way past. His fingers sank into the soft velour of her bathrobe as he turned her to face him. He could feel the slenderness of her arm in spite of the pillowy softness of the thick fabric, reminding him of how feminine she was. A hot coil of lust burned in his groin, winding tighter and tighter. 'I might've been a little rough on you downstairs earlier.'

Her brows lifted and she pulled out of his light hold. 'Might've been?'

He let out a whooshing breath. 'Okay, I *was* rough on you. I didn't think about how you'd be feeling about the break-up.'

'It's not a break-up. It's a *break*.'

Jake wasn't following the semantics. 'You don't think it's permanent?'

Her chin came up. 'No. Myles just needs a bit of space.'

He frowned. 'But what about us? Don't you

think he's going to get a little pissed you found someone else so soon?'

She looked at him as if he were wearing a dunce's cap. 'Yes, but that's the whole point. Sometimes people don't know what they've got until it's gone.'

'Has he called you since the news of our—' Jake couldn't help grimacing over the word '—engagement was announced?'

'Heaps of times but I'm not answering,' Jaz said. 'I'm letting him stew for a bit.'

'Do you think he believes it's true?'

'Why wouldn't he? Everyone else bought it. Apart from Julius, of course.'

'I'm surprised Miranda fell for it, to tell you the truth,' Jake said.

Jaz frowned. 'Why do you say that? Have you spoken to her?'

'She sent me a congratulatory text but I haven't spoken to her. I've been dodging her calls. But you're her closest friend. She'll suss something's amiss once she sees us together.'

Her lips compressed for a moment. 'I don't think it will be a problem. Anyway, she's busy with her own engagement and wedding plans.'

Jake studied her for a beat. 'Are you in love with this Myles guy?'

Her brow wrinkled. 'What sort of question is that? Of course I am.'

'Were you in love with Tim and Linton?'

'*Lincoln*,' she said with a scowl. 'Yes, I was.'

'You're pretty free and easy with your affection, aren't you?'

Jaz gave him a gelid look. 'That's rich coming from the man who changes partners faster than tyres are changed in a Formula One pit lane.'

Jake couldn't help smiling. 'You flatter me. I'm fast but not that fast.'

'Have you heard from Emma?'

'No.'

'So my plan is working.'

'So far.' He didn't like to admit it but there was no denying it. From being bombarded with texts, emails and calls there had been zilch from

Emma since Jasmine had delivered her bomb-
shell announcement. Another thing he didn't
like to acknowledge was how he'd had nothing
but congratulations from all his friends and col-
leagues. Even his parents had stopped slinging
insults at each other via the press long enough
to congratulate him. He had even had an email
from a client he'd thought he'd lost, promising
not just his business but that of several high-
profile contacts.

This little charade was turning out to be much
more of a win-win than Jake had expected.

'What we need is to be seen out in public,'
Jaz said. 'That will make it even more believ-
able.'

'In public?'

'Yes, like on a date or dinner or something.'

'You reckon we could get through a whole
meal together without you throwing something
at me?'

Her gaze moved out of reach of his. 'I'll do
my best.'

* * *

Jaz woke the next morning to a call from Miranda. 'I know it's early but I can't get Jake on his phone to congratulate him,' Miranda said. 'I figured he'd be in bed with you. Can you hand me to him? That is, if it's not inconvenient?' The way she said 'inconvenient' was playful and teasing.

Jaz swallowed back a gulp. 'Erm…he's having a shower right now. I'll get him to call you, okay?'

'Okay,' Miranda said. 'So how's it going? Does it seem real? I mean, for all this time you've been at each other's throats. Is it good to be making love instead of war?'

Jaz got out of bed but on her way to the window caught sight of her reflection in the mirror. How could she lie to her best friend? Lying by text was one thing. Lying in conversation was another. It didn't seem right. Not when they had been friends for so long. 'Miranda, listen, things aren't quite what they seem…I'm not really engaged to Jake. We're pretending.'

'*Pretending?*' Miranda sounded bitterly disappointed. 'But why?'

'I'm trying to win Myles back,' Jaz said. 'He wanted to take a break and I thought I'd try and make him jealous.'

'But why did Jake agree to it?' Miranda said.

'I didn't give him a choice.' Jaz explained the situation about Emma briefly.

'Gosh,' Miranda said. 'I was so excited for you. Now I feel like someone's punched me in the belly.'

'I'm sorry for lying but—'

'Are you sure about Myles?' Miranda said. 'I mean, *absolutely* sure he's the one?'

'Of course I'm sure. Why else would I be going to so much trouble to win him back?'

'Pride?'

Jaz pressed her lips together. 'It's not a matter of pride. It's a matter of love.'

'But you fall in and out of love all the time,' Miranda said. 'How do you know he's the right one for you when you could just as easily fall in love with someone else tomorrow?'

'I'm not going to fall in love with anyone else,' Jaz said. 'How can I when I'm in love with Myles?'

'What do you love about him?'

'We've had this conversation before and I—'

'Let's have it again,' Miranda said. 'Refresh my memory. List three things you love about him.'

'He's...'

'See?' Miranda said. 'You're hesitating!'

'Look, I know you don't like him, so it wouldn't matter what I said about him; you'd find some reason to discount it.'

'It's not that he's not nice and polite, handsome and well-educated and all that,' Miranda said. 'But I worry you only like him because you can control him. You've got a strong personality, Jaz. You need someone who'll stand up to you. Someone who'll be your equal, not your puppet.'

Jaz swung back from the window and paced the carpet. 'I don't like controlling men. I hate them. I always have and I always will. I could never fall in love with someone like that.'

'We'll see.'

She frowned. 'What do you mean, "we'll see"? I hope you're not thinking what I think you're thinking because it's not going to happen. No way.'

'Come on, Jaz,' Miranda said. 'You've had a thing for Jake since you were sixteen.'

'I was a kid back then!' Jaz said. 'It was just a stupid crush. I got over it, okay?'

'If you got over it then why have you avoided him like the black plague ever since?'

Jaz was close to Miranda but not close enough to tell her what had happened that night after she'd left Jake's room. She wasn't close enough to anyone to tell them that. Sharing that shame with someone else wouldn't make it go away. The only way she could make it go away was not to think about it. If she told anyone about it they would look at her differently. They might judge her. Blame her. She didn't want to take the risk. Her tough-girl façade was exactly that—a façade.

Underneath all the bravado she was still that terrified sixteen-year-old who had got herself sexually assaulted by a drunken guest at the party. It hadn't been rape but it had come scarily close to it. The irony was the person who did it had been so drunk they hadn't remembered a thing about it the following morning. The only way Jaz could deal with it was to pretend it hadn't happened. There was no other way. 'Look, I'm not avoiding Jake now, so you should be happy,' she said. 'Who knows? We might even end up friends after this charade is over.'

'I certainly hope so because I don't want Julius

and Holly's wedding, or mine and Leandro's, spoilt by you two looking daggers at each other,' Miranda said. 'It's bad enough with Mum and Dad carrying on World War Three.'

'That reminds me. Have you met Kat Winwood yet?' Jaz asked.

'No.' Miranda gave a sigh. 'She won't have anything to do with any of us. I guess if I were in her shoes I might feel the same. What Dad did to her mother was pretty unforgiveable.'

'Yes, well, paying someone to have an abortion isn't exactly how to win friends and influence people, I'll grant you that,' Jaz said.

'What about you?' Miranda said. 'You mentioned a couple of weeks back you were thinking about meeting her. Any luck?'

'Nope,' Jaz said. 'I might not be a Ravensdale but I'm considered close enough to your family to be on the black list as well.'

'Maybe Flynn can get her to change her mind,' Miranda said, referring to the family lawyer,

Flynn Carlyon, who had been a year ahead of Jake and Julius at school. 'If anyone can do it he can. He's unlikely to give up until he gets what he wants.'

'But I thought the whole idea was to get her to go away,' Jaz said. 'Wasn't that what Flynn was supposed to do? Pay her to keep from speaking to the press?'

'Yes, but she wouldn't take a penny off him. She hasn't said a word to the media anyway and it's been over a month,' Miranda said. 'Dad's agent called him last night about putting on a party to celebrate his sixty years in showbiz in January. Dad wants Kat there. He says he won't go ahead with it unless she comes.'

'Sixty years?' Jaz said. 'Gosh. What age did he start?'

'Five. He had a walk-on part in some musical way back. Hasn't he shown you the photos?'

'Nope,' Jaz said. 'I must've missed that bragging session.'

'Ha ha,' Miranda said. 'But what are we going to do about Kat? She has to come to Dad's party otherwise he'll be devastated.'

'Well, at least Flynn will have a few weeks to change her mind.'

'I can't work her out,' Miranda said. 'She's a struggling actor who's only had bit parts till now. You'd think she'd be jumping at the chance to cash in on her biological father's fame.'

'Maybe she needs time to get her head around who her father is,' Jaz said. 'It must've come as a huge shock finding out like that just before her mother died.'

'Yes, I guess so.' Miranda sighed again and then added, 'Are you sure you know what you're doing, Jaz—I mean with Jake? I can't help worrying this could backfire.'

'I know exactly what I'm doing,' Jaz said. 'I'm using Jake and he's using me.'

There was a telling little silence.

'You're not going to sleep with him, are you?' Miranda said.

Jaz laughed. 'I know he's your brother and all that but there are some women on this planet who can actually resist him, you know.'

And I had better keep on doing it.

Jake was coming back in from a morning run around the property when he saw Jaz coming down the stairs, presumably for breakfast. She was wearing light-grey yoga pants and a baby-girl pink slouch top that revealed the cap of a creamy shoulder and the thin black strap of her bra. Her slender feet were bare apart from liquorice-black toenail polish and her hair was in a messy knot on the top of her head that somehow managed to look casual and elegant at the same time. She wasn't wearing a sker-rick of make-up but if anything it made her look all the more breath-snatchingly beautiful. But then, since when had her stunning grey-blue eyes with their thick, spider-leg long lashes and prominent eyebrows needed any enhancement?

He caught a whiff of her bergamot-and-geranium essential oil as she came to stand on the last step, making her almost eye-to-eye with him. The urge to touch her lissom young body was overpowering. He had to curl his hands into fists to prevent himself from running a hand down the creamy silk of her cheek or tracing that gorgeous mouth with his finger.

Her eyes met his and a punch of lust slammed him in the groin. The fire and ice in that stormy sea of grey and blue had a potent impact on him. It happened every time their eyes collided. It was like a bolt of electricity zapping him, making everything that was male in him stand to attention. 'I told Miranda the truth about us,' she said with a touch of defiance.

Jake decided to wind her up a bit. 'That we have the hots for each other and are about to indulge in a passionate fling that's been seven years in the making?'

She folded her arms like a schoolmistress who was dealing with a particularly cheeky pupil, but he noticed her cheeks had gone a faint shade of pink. 'No,' she said as tartly as if she had just bitten into a lemon. 'I told her we aren't engaged and we still hate each other.'

He picked up a stray strand of hair that had escaped her makeshift knot and tucked it safely back behind the neat shell of her ear. He felt her give a tiny shiver as his fingers brushed the skin behind her ear and her mouth opened and closed as if she was trying to disguise her little involuntary gasp. 'You don't hate me, sweetheart. You *want* me.'

The twin pools of colour in her cheeks darkened another shade and her eyes flashed with livid blue-tipped flames. 'Do you get charged extra on flights for carrying your ego on board?'

Jake smiled crookedly as he trailed his fingertip from the crimson tide on her cheekbone to the neat hinge of her jaw. 'I see it every time you look at me. I feel it when I'm near you. You feel it too, don't you?'

The point of her tongue sneaked out over her lips in a darting movement. 'All I feel when I'm near you is the uncontrollable urge to scratch my nails down your face.'

He unpeeled one of her hands from where it was tucked in around her middle and laid it flat against his jaw. 'Go on,' he said, challenging her with his gaze. 'I won't stop you.'

Her hand was like cool silk against his skin. A shiver scooted down his spine as he felt the slight scrape of her nails against his morning stubble but then, instead of scoring his face, she began to stroke it. The sound of her soft skin moving over his raspy jaw had an unmistakably erotic element to it. Her touch sent a rocket blast through his pelvis and he put a hand at the base of her spine to draw her closer to his restless, urgent heat. The contact of her body so intimately against his was like fireworks exploding. His mouth came down in search of hers but he didn't have to go far as she met him more than halfway. Her soft lips were parted in anticipation, her vanilla-milkshake breath mingling with his for a spine-tingling microsecond before her mouth fused with his.

She gave a low moan of approval as he moved his mouth against hers, seeking her moist warmth with the stroke and glide of his tongue. She melted against him, her arms winding around his neck, her fingers delving through his hair, holding his head in place as if she was terrified he would pull back from her.

Jake had no intention of pulling back. He was enjoying the taste of her too much, the heat and unbridled passion that blossomed with every stroke and flicker of his tongue against hers. She pressed herself against him, her supple body fitting along his harder contours as if she had been fashioned just for him. He cupped her neat behind, holding her against the throbbing urgency of his arousal as his mouth fed hungrily off the sweet and drugging temptation of hers.

He lifted his mouth only far enough to change position but she grabbed at him, clamping her lips to his, her tongue darting into his mouth to mate wantonly with his. His blood pounded with excitement. His heart rate sped. His thighs fizzed with the need to take charge, to possess the hot, tight, wet vault of her body until this clawing, desperate need was finally satisfied.

Hadn't he always known she would be dynamite in his arms? Hadn't he always wanted to do this? Even that night when she'd been too young to know what she was doing. He had ached and burned to possess her then and he ached and burned now. One kiss wasn't going to be enough. It wasn't enough to satisfy the raging lust rippling through his body. He wanted to feel her convulsing around him as he took her to heaven and back. He knew they would be good together. He had always known it on some level. He felt it whenever their eyes met—the electric jolt of awareness that triggered something primitive in him.

Nothing would please him more than to see her gasping out his name as she came. Nothing would give him more pleasure than to have her admit she wanted him as much as he wanted her. To prove to her it wasn't her 'taking a break' fiancé she was hankering after but *him* she wanted. The man she had wanted since she was a teenager. The man she said she hated but lusted after like a forbidden drug. *That* was what he saw in her eyes—the desire she didn't want to feel but was there, simmering and smouldering with latent heat.

Jake slipped a hand under her loose top in search of the tempting globe of her breast. She hummed her pleasure against his lips as he moved her bra aside to make skin-on-skin contact. For years he had wanted to touch her like this—to feel her soft, creamy skin against his palm and hear her throatily express her need. He passed his thumb over her tightly budded nipple and then circled it before he bent his head and took it into his mouth. She gave another primal moan as he suckled on her breast, using the gentle scrape of his teeth and the sweep and salve of his tongue to tantalise her.

He slipped a hand down between their hard-pressed bodies, cupping her mound, his own body so worked up he wondered if he was going to jump the gun for the first time since he'd been a clumsy teenager.

But suddenly Jaz pulled back, pushing against his chest with the heels of her hands. 'Stop,' she said in a breathless-sounding voice. 'Please… stop.'

Jake held his hands up to show he was cool with her calling a halt. 'Your call, sweetheart.'

She pressed her lips together as she straightened her top, her hands fumbling and uncoordinated. 'You had no right to do that,' she said, shooting him a hard look.

He gave a lazy smile. 'Well, look who's talking. I wonder what lover boy would say if he'd been a fly on the wall just now? His devoted little "having a break" fiancée getting all hot and bothered with just a friendly kiss.'

Her eyes went to hairpin-thin slits. 'There was nothing friendly about it. You don't even like me. You just wanted to prove a point.'

'What point would that be?'

She tossed her head in an uppity manner as she turned to go back upstairs. 'I'm not having this conversation. You had no right to touch me and that's the end of it. Don't do it again.'

Jake waited until she was almost to the top of the stairs before he said, 'What about when we're out in public? Am I allowed to touch you then?'

A circle of ice rimmed her flattened mouth as she turned to glare at him. 'Only if it's absolutely necessary.'

He smiled a devilish smile. 'I'll look forward to it.'

CHAPTER FIVE

JAZ STORMED INTO her room and shut the door. She would have slammed it except she had already shown Jake how much he had rattled her. She didn't want to give his over-blown ego any more of a boost. She was furious with him for kissing her. How dared he take such liberties? A little voice reminded her that she hadn't exactly resisted but, on the contrary, had given him every indication she was enjoying every pulse-racing second of it.

Which she had been. Damn it.

His kiss had made her face what she didn't want to face. What she hadn't wanted to face for seven years. She wanted him. It was like it was programmed into her genes or something. He triggered something in her that no other man ever had. Her body sizzled when he was around. His touch created an earthquake of longing. How could a kiss make her feel so…so alive? It was crazy. Madness. Lunacy.

It was just like him to make a big joke about everything. This was nothing but a game to him. He enjoyed baiting her. Goading her. *Tempting* her. Why had she allowed him to get that close to her? She should have stepped back while she'd had the chance. Or maybe she hadn't had the chance because her body had other ideas. Wicked ideas that involved him touching her and pleasuring her in a way she had never quite felt before. Why had *his* touch made her flesh tingle and quake with delight? Why had *his* kiss made her heart race and her pulse thrum with longing?

It was just a kiss. It wasn't as if she hadn't been kissed before. She'd had plenty of kisses. Heaps. Dozens. Maybe hundreds… Well, maybe things had been a bit light on that just lately.

She couldn't quite recall the last time Myles had kissed her. Not properly. Not passionately, as if he couldn't get enough of her taste and touch. Over the last few weeks their kisses had turned into a rather perfunctory peck on the cheek at hello and goodbye. And as to touching her breasts, well, Myles wasn't good at breasts. He didn't seem to understand she didn't like being pinched or squeezed, like he was someone checking a piece of fruit for ripeness.

Jaz let out a frustrated breath. Why did Jake have to be the expert on kissing her and handling her breasts? It wasn't fair. She didn't want him to have such sensual power over her. He could turn her on by just looking at her with that glinting dark gaze.

Of course it would be *so* much worse now. Now he had actually kissed her and touched her breasts and her lady land. God, she'd almost come on the spot when he'd cupped her down there. How could one man's touch have such an effect on her? She didn't even like him. She loathed him. He was her arch-enemy. He wasn't just a thorn in her side. He was the whole damn rose bush. Unpruned. He was everything she avoided in a partner.

But he sure could kiss. Jaz had to give him that. His lips had done things to hers no man had ever done before. His tongue had lit a blazing fire in her core and it hadn't gone out. The hot coals were smouldering there even now. Her body felt restless. Feverish. Hungry. Starving for more of his electrifying caresses. What would it feel like to have him deep inside her? Moving in her body in that hectic rush for release?

Sex had always been a complicated issue for her. She put it down to the fact her first experience of it had been so twisted and tangled up with shame. She had taken a drink from a young man at the party, more to get back at Jake for rejecting her. She had flirted with the man, hoping Jake would see that not all men found her repulsive. But she hadn't factored in the amount of alcohol she had already consumed or her over-wrought emotional state. She couldn't quite re-member how she had ended up in one of the downstairs bathrooms with the man, sweaty and smelling of wine as he tore at her clothes and groped and slobbered all over her until she'd finally got away. All she could remember was the shame—the sickening shame of not being in control.

Now whenever she had sex that same shame lurked at the back of her mind. Although she en-joyed some aspects of making love—the touch-ing and being needed—she hadn't always been able to relax enough to orgasm. Not that any of her partners had seemed to notice. She might not be a proper Ravensdale but she sure could act when she needed to. Pretending to orgasm every time hadn't been her intention. But once had turned into twice and then it had been far easier than explaining.

How could she explain her behaviour that night? The rational part of her knew the man at the party had some responsibility to acquire proper consent before he touched her, but how did she know if she'd given it or not? It would be his word against hers, that was, if he'd actually remembered. She'd seen him the next morning as the overnight guests were leaving but he had looked right through her as if he had never seen her before. Had she agreed to kiss him in the bathroom or had he come in on her and seized the opportunity to assault her? She didn't know and it was the not knowing that was the most shameful thing for her.

Jaz wasn't into victim blaming but when it came to herself she struggled to forgive herself for allowing something like that to happen. She had buried her shame behind a 'don't mess with me' façade and a sharp tongue but deep inside she was still that shocked and terrified girl.

And she had a scary feeling if she spent too much time alone with Jake Ravensdale he would begin to see it.

* * *

Jaz was doing some work on Holly's dress in her room and when her phone rang she picked it up without thinking. 'Jasmine Connolly.'

'Jaz. Finally you answered,' Myles said. 'Why on earth haven't you returned my calls?'

'Oh, hi, Myles,' she said breezily. 'How are you?'

He released a whooshing breath. 'How do you think I am? I turn my back for a moment and my fiancée is suddenly engaged to someone else.'

Jaz smiled as she put her needle and thread down. It was working. It was actually working. Myles was insanely jealous. She had never heard him speak so possessively before. 'You were the one who suggested we take a break.'

'Yes, but dating other people is not the same as getting engaged to them. We'd only been apart twenty-four hours and you hooked up with him. No one falls in love that quickly. No one, and especially not Jake bloody Ravensdale.'

Jaz hadn't really taken in that bit. The bit where Myles had said they were free to date other people. She'd thought he was just having some breathing space. Her 'engagement' to Jake wouldn't have the same power if Myles was seeing someone else. What if he fell in love? What if *he* got engaged to someone else? 'Are you seeing other people?'

There was a short silence.

'I had a drink with an old friend but I haven't got myself bloody engaged to them,' he said in a sulky tone.

Jaz twirled a tendril of her hair around her finger as she walked about the room with the phone pressed to her ear. How cool was this, hearing Myles sound all wounded and affronted by her moving on so quickly? Didn't that prove he still loved her? The irony was he'd been the first to say those three magical little words. But he hadn't said it for weeks. Months, even. But a couple more weeks of having Jake Ravensdale brandished in his face would do the trick. Myles would soon be begging her to take him back. 'I have to go,' she said. 'Jake is taking me out to dinner.'

'I give it a week,' Myles said. 'Two at the most. He won't stick around any longer than that. You mark my words.'

Two is all I need. The winter wedding expo in the Cotswolds was the coming weekend. It was her stepping stone to the big time. She hoped to expand her business and what better way than to attend with a heart-stopping, handsome fiancé in tow? There was no way she wanted to go alone. She would look tragic if she went without a fiancé. She couldn't bear to be considered a fraud, making 'happy ever after' dresses but failing to find love herself. But if she took Jake Ravensdale as her fiancé —the poster boy for pick-ups—it would give her serious street cred. Besides, it would be the perfect payback to him for humiliating her. It would be unmitigated torture for commitment-phobe Jake to be dragged around a ballroom full of wedding finery.

She smiled a secret smile. Yes, staying 'engaged' to Jake suited her just fine.

Jake was scrolling through his emails in the library—thankfully none were from Emma Madden—when Jaz came sashaying in, bringing with her the scent of flowers and temptation. His body sprang to attention when she approached the desk where he was sitting. She had changed out of her yoga pants and top and was now wearing skin-tight jeans, knee-length leather boots and a baby-blue cashmere sweater with a patterned scarf artfully gathered around her slim neck. Her honey-brown hair was loose about her shoulders and her beautiful mouth was glistening with lip-gloss, drawing his gaze like a magnet. He could still taste her. Could still feel the way her tongue had danced with his in sensual heat. He saw her gaze drift to his mouth as if she were recalling that erotic interlude. 'Forgiven me yet?' he said.

She tossed her hair back over her shoulders in a haughty manner, giving him an ice-cool glare. 'For?'

'You know exactly what for.'

She shifted her gaze, picked a pen off the desk and turned it over in her slender hands as if it was something of enormous interest to her. 'I was wondering what you're up to next weekend.'

He leaned back in the leather chair and balanced one ankle over his thigh. 'My calendar is pretty heavily booked. What did you have in mind?'

Her grey-blue eyes came back to his. 'I have a function I need to attend in Gloucester. I was hoping you'd come with me—you know, to keep up appearances.'

'What sort of function?'

'Just a drinks thing.'

Jake steepled his fingers against his nose and

mouth. The little minx was up to something but he would play along. He might even get another kiss or two out of her. 'Sure, why not?'

She put the pen down. 'I'm going to head back to London now.'

He felt a swooping sensation of disappointment in his gut. It would be deadly boring staying here without her to spar with. They hadn't had any time together without anyone else around for years. He hadn't realised how much he was enjoying it until the prospect of it ending now loomed. But there would be other opportunities as long as this charade continued. And he was going to make the most of them. 'You're not staying till morning?'

'No, I have stuff to do at the boutique first thing and I don't want to get caught up in traffic.'

Jake suspected she was wary of spending any more time with him in case she betrayed her desire for him. He wasn't being overly smug about it. He could see it as plain as day. It mirrored his raging lust for her. Not that he was going to act on it but it sure was a heap of fun making her think he was. 'Are you going to see Myles?'

Her gaze slipped out of reach of his. 'Not yet. We agreed on a month's break.'

'A lot can happen in a month.'

Her lips tightened as if she was trying to remove the sensation of his on them. 'I know what I'm doing.'

'Do you?'

Her eyes clashed with his. 'I know you think relationships are a complete waste of time but commitment is important to me.'

'He's not the right man for you,' Jake said.

Her hands went to her slim hips in a combative pose. 'And I suppose you think you're an expert on who exactly would be?'

He pushed back his chair to come around to her side of the desk. She took half a step backwards but the antique globe was in the way. Her eyes drifted to his mouth and her darting tongue took a layer of lip-gloss off her lips. 'If Myles was the right man for you he'd be down here right now with his hands at my throat.'

Her eyes glittered with enmity. 'Not all men resort to Neanderthal tactics to claim a partner.'

He took a fistful of her silky hair and gently anchored her. 'If I was in love with you I would do whatever it took to get you back.'

Her eyelids went to half-mast as her gaze zeroed in on his mouth for a moment. 'Men like you don't know the meaning of the word love. Lust is the only currency you deal in.'

Jake glided his hand down from her hair to cup her cheek, his thumb moving over the creamy perfection of her skin like the slow arm of a metronome. He watched as her pupils enlarged like widening pools of black ink, her mouth parting, her soft, milky breath coming out in a soundless gasp. 'There's nothing wrong with a bit of lust. It's the litmus test of a good relationship.'

'You don't have relationships,' she said, still looking at his mouth. 'You have encounters that don't last longer than it takes to change a light bulb.'

He gave a slanted smile. 'Who needs a light bulb when we've got this sort of electricity going on?'

She pursed her lips. 'Don't even think about it.'

He brushed his thumb across her bunched up lips. 'I think about it all the time. How it would feel to have you scraping your nails down my back as I make you come.'

She gave a tiny shudder. Blinked. Swallowed. 'I'd much rather scrape them down your arrogant face.'

Jake smiled. 'Liar. You're thinking about it now, aren't you? You're thinking about how hot I make you feel. How turned on. I bet if I slipped my fingers into you now you'd be dripping wet for me.'

Twin pools of pink flagged her cheekbones. 'It's not going to happen, Jake,' she said through tight lips. 'I'm engaged to another man.'

'Maybe you'll feel different once you're wearing my ring. I'll pick you up at lunchtime tomorrow at the boutique. Be ready at two p.m.'

Her eyes flashed with venom. 'I have an appointment with a client.'

'Cancel it.'

She looked as if she was going to argue the point but then she blew out a hiss of a breath and stormed out of the room, slamming the door behind her for good measure.

Barely a minute later he heard her car start with a roar and then the scream of her tyres as she flew down the driveway.

He smiled and turned back to his laptop. *Yep. A heap of fun.*

CHAPTER SIX

JAZ HAD JUST finished with a customer who had purchased one of her hand-embroidered veils for her daughter when Jake came into the boutique. The woman smiled up at him as he politely held the door open for her. 'Thank you,' she said. 'I hear congratulations are in order. You've got yourself a keeper there.' She nodded towards Jaz. 'She'll make a gorgeous bride. When's the big day?'

Jake smiled one of his laidback smiles. 'We haven't set a date yet, have we, sweetheart?'

'No, not yet,' Jaz said.

'I can't wait to see the ring,' the woman said. 'I bet you'll give her a big one.'

Jake's dark-blue eyes glinted as they glanced at Jaz. 'You bet I will.'

Jaz felt a tremor go through her private parts at his innuendo. Did the man have no shame? She was trying to act as cool and professional as she could and one look at her from those glittering midnight-blue eyes and she felt like she was going to melt into a sizzling pool at his feet. She wouldn't have mentioned anything about their 'engagement' to the customer but it seemed there wasn't a person in the whole of London who hadn't heard fast-living playboy Jake Ravensdale was getting himself hitched.

The woman left with a little wave, and the door with its tinkling bell closed. Jake came towards the counter where Jaz had barricaded herself. 'So this is your stamping ground,' he said, glancing around at the dresses hanging on the free-standing rack. 'How much of a profit are you turning over?'

She gave him a flinty look. 'I don't need you to pull apart my business.'

His one-shoulder shrug was nonchalant. 'Just asking.'

'You're not just asking,' Jaz said. 'You're looking for an opportunity to tell me I'm rubbish at running my business, just like you keep pointing out how rubbish I am at running my personal life.'

'You have to admit three engagements—four, if you count ours—is a lot of bad decisions.'

She gripped the edge of the counter. 'And I suppose you've never made a bad decision in the whole of your charmed life, have you?'

'I've made a few.'

'Such as?'

He looked at her for a long moment, his customary smile fading and a slight frown taking its place. 'It was crass of me to bring those girls to my room that night. There were other ways I could've handled the situation.'

Jaz refused to be taken in by an admission

of regret seven years too late. 'Did you sleep with them?'

'No.'

There was a pregnant pause.

'Where did you go after that?' he said. 'I didn't see you for the rest of the night.'

Jaz looked down at the glass-topped counter where all the garters were arranged. 'I went back to my room.'

He reached across the counter to take one of her hands in his. 'Look at me, Jasmine.'

She slowly brought her gaze up to his, affecting the expression of a bored teenager preparing for a stern lecture from a parent. 'What?'

His eyes moved between each of hers as if he was searching for something hidden behind the cool screen of her gaze. She could feel the warm press of his hand against hers, his long, strong, masculine fingers entwining with hers, making her insides slip and shift. She could smell the sharp citrus of his aftershave. She could see the dark shadow of his regrowth peppered along his jaw. She could see every fine line on his mouth, the way his lips were set in a serious line—such a change from his usual teasing slant. He began to move the pad of his thumb in a stroking fashion over the back of her hand, the movements drugging her senses.

'It wasn't that I wasn't attracted to you,' he said. 'I just didn't want to make things awkward with you being such a part of the family. That and the fact you were too young to know what you were doing.'

Jaz pulled her hand away. 'Then why lead me on as if you were serious about me? That was just plain cruel.'

He let out a deep sigh. 'Yeah, I guess it was.'

She studied his features for a moment, wondering if this too was an act. How could she believe he was sorry for how he'd made her think he was falling in love with her? He had been so charming towards her, telling her how beautiful she was and how he couldn't wait to get her alone. She had fallen for every lie, waiting in his room, undressing down to her underwear for him in her haste to do anything she could to please him. She had been too emotionally immature to realise he had been winding her up. She had been too enamoured with him to see his charm offensive for what it was. He had pulled her strings like a puppet master. Hating him was dead easy when he wasn't sorry for how he'd treated her. For the last seven years she had stoked that hatred with every look or cynical lip curl he aimed her way. But if this apology were genuine she would have to let her anger and hatred go.

That was scary.

Her anger was a barrier. A big, fat barricade around her heart because falling in love with Jake would be nothing less than an exercise in self-annihilation. She only fell in love with men she knew for certain would love her back. Her ex-fiancés were alike in that they had each been comfortable with commitment. They'd wanted the same things she wanted…or so they had said.

Jake glanced at his watch. 'We'd better get a move on. I made an appointment with the jeweller for two-fifteen. Have you got an assistant to hold the fort for you till you get back?'

'No, my last girl was rude to the clients,' Jaz said. 'I had to let her go. I haven't got around to replacing her. I'll just put a "back in ten minutes" sign on the door.'

He frowned. 'You mean you run this show all by yourself?'

She picked up her purse and jacket from underneath the counter. 'I outsource some of the cutting and sewing but I do most of everything else because that's what my customers expect.'

'But none of the top designers do all the hack work,' Jake said as they walked out of the boutique into the chilly autumn air. 'You'll burn yourself out trying to do everything yourself.'

'Yes, well, I'm not quite pulling in the same profit as some of those houses,' Jaz said. 'But watch this space. I have a career plan.'

'What about a business plan? I could have a look at your company structure and—'

'No thanks,' Jaz said and closed and locked the boutique door.

'If you're worried about my fee, I could do mate's rates.'

She gave him a sideways look. 'I can afford you, Jake. I just choose not to use your...erm... services.'

He shrugged one of his broad shoulders. 'Your loss.'

The jeweller was a private designer who had a studio above an interior design shop. Jaz was acutely conscious of Jake's arm at her elbow as he led her into the viewing area. After brief introductions were made a variety of designs was brought forward for her to peruse. But there was one ring that was a stand out. It was a mosaic collection of diamonds in an art deco design that was both simple yet elegant. She slipped it on her finger and was pleased to find it was a perfect fit. 'This one,' she said, holding it up to see the way the light bounced off the diamonds.

'Good choice,' the designer said. 'It suits your hand.'

Jaz didn't see the price. It wasn't the sort of jeweller where price tags were on show. But she didn't care if it was expensive or not. Jake could afford it. She did wonder, however, if he would want her to give it back when their 'engagement' was over.

Jake took her hand as they left the studio. 'Fancy a quick coffee?'

Jaz would have said no except she hadn't had lunch and her stomach was gurgling like a drain. 'Sure, why not?'

He took her to a café a couple of blocks from her boutique but they had barely sat down before someone from a neighbouring table took a photo of them with a camera phone. Then a murmur went around the café and other people started aiming their phones at them. Jaz tried to keep her smile natural but her jaw was aching from the effort. Jake seemed to take it all in his stride, however.

One customer came over with a napkin and a pen. 'Can I have your autograph, Jake?'

Jake slashed his signature across the napkin and handed back the pen with an easy smile. 'There you go.'

'Is it true you and Miss Connolly are engaged?' the customer asked.

Jaz held up her ring hand. 'Yes. We just picked up the ring.'

More cameras went off and the Twitter whistle sounded so often it was as if a flock of small birds had been let loose in the café.

'Nice work,' Jake said when the fuss had finally died down a little.

'You were the one who suggested a coffee,' Jaz said, shooting him a look from beneath her lashes.

'I heard your stomach rumbling at the jeweller's.Don't you make time for lunch?'

She stirred her latte with a teaspoon rather than lose herself in his sapphire-blue gaze. 'I've got a lot on just now.'

He reached across the table and took her left hand in his, running his fingertip over the crest of the mosaic ring. 'You can keep it after this is over.'

Jaz brought her gaze back to his. 'You don't want to recycle it for when you eventually settle down?'

He released her hand and sat back as he gave a light laugh. 'Can you see me doing the school run?'

'You don't ever want kids?'

'Nope,' he said, reaching for the sugar and tipping two teaspoons in. 'I don't want the responsibility. If I'm going to screw anyone's life up, it'll be my own. *That* I can live with.'

'Why do you think you'd screw up your children's lives?' Jaz said.

He stirred his coffee before he answered. 'I'm too much like my father.'

'I don't think you're anything like your father,' she said. 'Maybe in looks but not in temperament. Your father is weak. Sorry if I'm speaking out of turn but he is. The way he handled his affair with Kat Winwood's mother is proof of it. I can't see you paying someone to have an abortion if you got a girl pregnant.'

He shifted his lips from side to side. 'I wouldn't offer to marry her, though.'

'Maybe not, but you'd support her and your child,' Jaz said. 'And you'd be involved in your child's life.'

He gave her one of his slow smiles that did so much damage to her resolve to keep him at a distance. 'I didn't realise you had such a high opinion of me.'

She pursed her lips. 'Don't get too excited. I still think you'd make a terrible husband.'

'In general or for you?'

Jaz looked at him for a beat or two of silence. She had a sudden vision of him at the end of the aisle waiting for her with that twinkling smile on his handsome face. Of his tall and toned body dressed in a sharply tailored suit instead of the casual clothes he preferred. Of his dark-blue eyes focused on her, as if she were the only woman he ever wanted to gaze at, with complete love and adoration.

She blinked and refocused. 'Good Lord, not for me,' she said with a laugh. 'We'd be at each other's throats before we left the church.'

Something moved at the back of his gaze as it held hers, a flicker like a faulty light bulb. But then he picked up his coffee cup and drained it before putting it down on the table with a decisive clunk. 'Ready?'

Jake walked Jaz back to the boutique holding her hand for the sake of appearances. Or so he told himself. The truth was he loved the feel of her small, neat hand encased in his. He couldn't stop himself from thinking about those soft, clever little fingers on other parts of his body. Stroking him, teasing him with her touch. Why shouldn't he make the most of their situation? He had a business deal to secure and being engaged to Jasmine Connolly was going to win him some serious brownie points with his conservative client Bruce Parnell. It wasn't as if it was for ever. A week or two and it would be over. Life would go back to normal.

'I have a work function on Wednesday night,' he said when Jaz had unlocked the door of the boutique. 'Dinner with a client. Would you like to come?'

She looked at him with a slight frown. 'Why?'

He tugged a tendril of her hair in a teasing manner. 'Because we're madly in love and we can't bear to be apart for a second.'

Her frown deepened and a flash of irritation arced in her gaze. 'What's the dress code?'

'Lounge suit and cocktail.'

'I'll have to check my calendar.'

Jake put his hand beneath her chin and tipped up her face so her eyes couldn't escape his. 'I'm giving you the weekend for the wedding expo. The least you could do is give me one week night.'

Her cheeks swarmed with sheepish colour. 'How did you know it was a wedding expo?'

He gave her a teasing grin. 'I knew there had to be a catch. Why else would you want me for a whole weekend?'

Her mouth took on that disapproving school-marm, pursed look that made him want to kiss it back into pliable softness. 'I don't want *you*, Jake. You'll only be there for show.'

He bent down and pressed a brief kiss to her mouth. 'I'll pick you up from here at seven.'

Jaz was still doing her hair when the doorbell sounded on Wednesday evening. She had run late with a client who had taken hours to choose a design for a gown. She gave her hair one last blast with the dryer and shook her head to let the waves fall loosely about her shoulders. She smoothed her hands down her hips, turning to one side to check her appearance in the full-length mirror. The black cocktail dress had double shoestring straps that criss-crossed over her shoulders, the silky fabric skimming her figure in all the right places. She was wearing her highest heels because she hadn't been able to wear them when going out with Myles, as he was only an inch taller than her. A quick spray of perfume and a smear of lip-gloss and she was ready.

Why she was going to so much trouble for Jake was not something she wanted to examine too closely. But when she opened the door and she saw the way his eyes ran over her appreciatively she was pleased she had chosen to go with the wow factor.

But then, so had he. He was dressed in a beautifully tailored suit that made his shoulders seem all the broader and, while he wasn't wearing a tie, the white open-necked shirt combined with the dark blue of his suit intensified the navy-blue of his eyes.

Jaz opened the door a little wider. 'I'll just get my wrap.'

Jake stepped into her flat and closed the door. She turned to face him as she draped her wrap over her shoulders, a little shiver coursing over her flesh as she saw the way his gaze went to her mouth as if pulled there by a powerful magnet.

The air quickened the way it always did when they were alone.

'Is something wrong?' she said.

He closed the small distance between their bodies so that they were almost touching. 'I have something for you,' he said, reaching into the inside pocket of his jacket.

Jaz swallowed as he took out a narrow velvet jewellery case the same colour as his eyes. She took it from him and opened it with fingers that were suddenly as useless as a glove without a hand. Jake took it from her and deftly opened it to reveal a stunning diamond pendant on a white-gold chain that was as fine as a gossamer thread.

Jaz glanced up at him but his face was unreadable. She looked back at the diamond. She had jewellery. Lots of it. Most of it she had bought herself because jewellery was so personal, a bit like perfume and make-up. She hadn't had a partner yet who had ever got her taste in jewellery right. But this was...perfect. She would have chosen it herself if she could have afforded it. She knew it was expensive. Hideously so. Why had Jake spent so much money on her when he didn't even like her? 'I'll give it back once we're done,' she said. 'And the ring.'

'I chose it specifically for you,' he said, taking it out of the box. 'Turn around. Move your hair out of the way.'

Jaz did as he commanded and tried not to shudder in pleasure as his long strong fingers moved against the sensitive skin on the back of her neck as he secured the pendant in place. She could feel the tall, hard frame of his body against her shoulder blades, his strongly muscled thighs against her trembling ones. She knew if she leaned back even half an inch she could come into contact with the hot, hard heat of him. She felt his hands come down on the tops of her shoulders, his fingers giving her a light squeeze as he turned her to face him. She looked into the midnight blue of his inscrutable gaze and wondered if her teenage crush was dead and buried after all. It felt like it was coming to life under the warm press of his hands on her body.

He trailed a lazy fingertip from beneath her ear to her mouth, circling it without touching it. But it felt like he had. Her lips buzzed, fizzed and ached for the pressure of his. 'You look beautiful.'

'Amazing what a flashy bit of jewellery can do.'

He frowned as if her flippant comment annoyed him. 'You don't suit flashy jewellery and

I wouldn't insult you by insisting on you wearing it.'

'All the same, I don't expect you to spend so much money on me. I don't feel comfortable about it, given our relationship.'

His eyes went to her mouth for a moment before meshing with hers. 'Why do you hate me so much?'

Jaz couldn't hold his gaze and looked at the open neck of his shirt instead. But that just made it worse because she could see the long, strong, tanned column of his throat and smell the light but intoxicating lemony scent of his aftershave. She didn't know if it was the diamond olive branch he had offered her, his physical closeness or both that made her decide to tell him the truth about that night. Or maybe it was because she was tired of the negative emotion weighing her down. 'That night after I left your room… I… Something happened…'

Jaz felt rather than saw his frown. She was still

looking at his neck but she noticed the way he had swallowed thickly. 'What?' he said.

'I accepted a drink off one of the guests. I'm not sure who it was. One of the casual seasonal theatre staff, I think. I hadn't seen him before or since. I was upset after leaving you. I didn't care if I got drunk. But then…I, well, you've probably heard it dozens of times before. Girls who get drunk and then end up regretting what happened next.'

'What happened next?' Jake's voice sounded raw, as if something had been scraped across his vocal chords.

Jaz still couldn't meet his gaze. She couldn't bear to see his judgement, his criticism of her reckless behaviour. 'I had a non-consensual encounter. Or at least I think it was non-consensual.'

'You were…*raped*?'

She looked at him then. 'No, but it was close to it. Somehow I managed to fight him off, but I was too ashamed to tell anyone what happened. I didn't even tell Miranda. I haven't told anyone before now.'

Jake's expression was full of outrage, shock and horror. 'The man should've been charged. Do you think you'd recognise him if you saw him again? We could arrange a police line-up. We could check the guest list of that night. Track down everyone who attended...'

Jaz pulled out from under his hold and crossed her arms over her body. 'No. I don't want to even think about that night. I don't even know if I gave the guy the okay to mess around. I was the one who started flirting with him in the first place. But then things got a little hazy. It would be his word against mine and you know what the defence lawyers would make of that. I was too drunk to know what I was doing.'

'But he might've spiked your drink or something,' Jake said. 'He committed a crime. A crime for which he should be punished.'

'That only happens in the movies,' Jaz said.

'I've moved on. It would make things so much harder for me if I had to revisit that night in a courtroom.'

His frown made a road map of lines on his forehead. 'I can see why you hate me so much. I'm as guilty as that lowlife.'

'No,' she said. 'That's not true.'

'Isn't it?'

Jaz bit her lip. 'I know it looks like I've blamed you all this time but that's just the projection of negative emotion. I guess I used you as a punching bag because I felt so ashamed.'

Jake came over to her and took her hands from where they were wrapped around her body, holding them gently in his. 'You have no need to be ashamed, Jaz. You were just a kid. I was the adult and I acted appallingly. I shouldn't have given you any encouragement. Leading you on like that only to throw those girls in your face was wrong. I should've been straight with you right from the get-go.'

Jaz gave him a wobbly smile. 'You just called me Jaz. You haven't done that in years.'

His hands gave hers a gentle squeeze. 'We'd better get a move on. My client isn't the most patient of men. That is if you're still okay with going? I can always tell him you had something on and go by myself.'

'I'm fine,' she said. And she was surprised to find it was true. Having Jake of all people being so understanding, caring and protective made something hard and tight inside her chest loosen like a knotted rope suddenly being released.

He gently grazed her cheek with the backs of his knuckles. 'Thank you for telling me.'

'I'd rather you didn't tell anyone else,' Jaz said. 'I don't want people to look at me differently.'

'Not even Miranda?'

She pulled at her lip with her teeth. 'Miranda would be hurt if I told her now. She'd blame herself for not watching out for me. You know what a little mother hen she is.'

Jake's frown was back. 'But surely—?'

'No,' Jaz said, sending him a determined look. 'Don't make me regret telling you. Promise me you won't betray my trust.'

He let out a frustrated sigh. 'I promise. But I swear to God, if I find out who hurt you I'll tear him apart with my bare hands.'

CHAPTER SEVEN

LATER, IN THE car going back to Jaz's place, Jake wondered how on earth he'd swung the deal with his client. His mind hadn't been on the game the whole way through dinner. All he'd been able to think about was what Jaz had told him about that wretched night after she had left his room. He was so churned up with a toxic cocktail of anger, guilt and an unnerving desire for revenge that he'd given his client, Bruce Parnell, the impression he was a distracted, lovesick fool rather than a savvy businessman. But that didn't seem to matter because at the end of the dinner his client had signed on the dotted line and wished Jake and Jaz all the best for their future.

Their future.

What *was* their future?

Jake was so used to bickering with her that he wasn't sure how he was going to navigate being friends with her instead. While it had been pistols and pissy looks at dawn, he'd been able to keep his distance. But now she'd shared her painful secret with him he couldn't carry on as if nothing had changed. Everything had changed. The whole dynamic of their relationship was different. He wanted to protect her. To fix it for her. To give her back her innocence so she didn't have to carry around the shame she felt. A shame she had no need to feel because the jerk who had assaulted her was the one who should be ashamed.

But Jake too felt shame. Deep, gut-clawing shame. Shame that he hadn't handled her infatuation with him more sensitively. His actions had propelled her into danger—danger that could have been avoided if he had been a little more understanding. He could see now why Jaz had stepped in with the engagement charade when Emma Madden had turned up at the door. She had been sensitive to the girl's need for dignity, offering her a safe way home with someone at the other end to make sure she was all right.

What had *he* done? He had sent Jaz from his room in an acute state of public humiliation only to fall into the hands of some creep who'd plied her with drink and drugs and God knew what else. Had that been her first experience of sex— being groped and manhandled by a drunken idiot? He couldn't remember if she'd had a boyfriend back then. Miranda had been going out with Mark Redbank from a young age but Jaz had never seemed all that interested in boys. Not until she'd developed that crush on him.

He couldn't bear the thought of her being touched in such a despicable way. Was that why she only ever dated men she could control? None of her ex-fiancés were what one would even loosely consider as alpha men. Was that deliberate or unconscious on her part?

Jake glanced at her sitting quietly in the passenger seat beside him. She was looking out at the rain-lashed street, her hands absently fiddling with the clasp on her evening bag. 'You okay?' he said.

She turned her head to look at him, a vacant smile on her face. 'Sorry. I think I used up all my scintillating conversation at dinner.'

'You did a great job,' Jake said. 'Bruce Parnell was quite taken with you. He was being cagey about signing up with me but you had him at hello.'

'Did you know he fell in love with his late wife the very first time they met? And they married three months later and never spent more than two nights apart for the whole of their marriage? He would fly back by private jet if he had to just to be with her.'

He glanced at her again between gear changes. 'He told you all that?'

'And he's still grieving her loss even though

it's been ten years. It reminded me of Miranda after Mark died.'

'Luckily Leandro got her to change her mind,' Jake said. 'I was sure she was going to end up a spinster living with a hundred cats.'

Jaz gave a tinkling laugh. 'I was worried too, but they're perfect for each other. I've known it for ages. It was the way Leandro looked at her. He got this really soft look in his eyes.'

Jake grunted. 'Another one bites the dust.'

'What have you got against marriage? It doesn't always end badly. Look at Mr Parnell.'

'That sort of marriage is the exception,' Jake said. 'Look at my parents. They're heading for another show-stopping divorce as far as I can tell. It was bad enough the first time.'

'Clearly Julius doesn't hold the same view as you,' she said. 'And yet he went through the same experience of your parents' divorce.'

'It was different for Julius,' Jake said. 'He found solace in studying and working hard.

I found it hard to adjust to boarding school. I pushed against the boundaries. Rubbed the teachers up the wrong way. Wasted their time and my own.'

'But you've done so well for yourself. Aren't you happy with your achievements?'

Was he happy? Up until a few days ago he had been perfectly happy. But now there was a niggling doubt chewing at the edge of his conscience. He moved around so much it was hard to know where was home. He had a base in London but most of the time he lived out of hotel rooms. He never cooked at home. He ate out. He didn't spend the night with anyone because he hated morning-after scenes. He didn't do reruns. One night was enough to scratch the itch. But how long could he keep on moving? The fast lane was a lonely place at times. Not that he was going to admit that to Jaz—or to anyone, when it came to that.

But this recent drama with Emma Madden had

got him thinking. Everyone saw him as shallow and self-serving. He hadn't given a toss for anyone's opinion before now but now it sat uncomfortably on him like an ill-fitting jacket. What if people thought he was like the man who had groped Jaz? That he was taking advantage of young women who were a little star-struck. It had never concerned him before. He had always enjoyed exploiting his parents' fame. He had used it to open doors in business and in pleasure. But how long could he go on doing it? He was turning into a cliché. The busty blondes he attracted only wanted him because he was good looking and had famous parents. They didn't know him as a person.

Jake pulled up outside Jaz's flat above her boutique. 'How long have you been living above the shop?' he asked as he walked her to the door.

She gave him a wary look. 'Is this another "how to run your business" lecture?'

'It's a nice place but pretty small. And the

whole living and working in the same place can be a drag after a while.'

'Yes, well, I was planning to move in with Myles but he put the brakes on that,' she said, scowling. 'His parents don't like me. They think I'm too pushy and controlling. I think that's the main reason he wanted a break.'

What's not to like? What parents wouldn't be proud to have her as their daughter-in-law? She was smart and funny, and sweet when she let her guard down. His parents were delighted with their 'engagement'. He hadn't figured out yet how he was going to tell them when it was over. They would probably never speak to him again. 'Do you really want to take Myles back?'

Her chin came up. 'Of course.'

'What if he doesn't want to come back?'

She averted her gaze. 'I deal with that *if* it happens.'

Jake looked at her for a long beat. 'You're not in love with him.'

Her eyes flashed back to his. 'And you know this how?'

'Because you're more concerned about what other people think of you than what he does. That's what this thing between us is all about. You're trying to save face, not your relationship.'

She flattened her lips so much they disappeared inside her mouth. 'I know what I'm doing. I know Myles better than anyone.'

'If you know him so well why haven't you told him about that night?'

She flinched as if he had struck her. But then she pulled herself upright as if her spinal column were filling with concrete. 'Thank you for dinner,' she said. 'Good night.'

'Jaz, wait—'

But the only response he got was the door being slammed in his face.

Jaz was at the boutique the next morning when Miranda came in carrying coffee and muffins.

'I thought I'd drop in to start the ball rolling on my wed—' Miranda said, but stopped short when her gaze went to Jaz's ring hand. 'Oh, my God. Did Jake buy that for you?'

'Yes, but it's just for show.'

Miranda snatched up Jaz's hand and turned it every which way to see how the light danced off the diamonds. 'Wow. I didn't realise he had such good taste in rings *and* in women.'

Jaz gave her a speaking look. 'You do realise none of this is for real?'

Miranda's eyes twinkled. 'So you both say, but I was just at Jake's office and he's like a bear with a sore paw. Did you guys have a tiff?'

'That's nothing out of the normal,' Jaz said, taking her coffee out of the cardboard holder.

Miranda cocked her head like an inquisitive bird. 'What's wrong?'

'Nothing. We just argued…about stuff.'

'All couples argue,' Miranda said. 'It's normal and healthy.'

'We're *not* a couple,' Jaz said. 'We're an act.'

Miranda frowned. 'You're not seriously still thinking of going back to Myles?'

Jaz pushed back from her work table. 'That's the plan.'

'It's a dumb plan,' Miranda said. 'A stupid plan that's totally wrong for you and for Myles. Can't you see that? You're not in love with him. You're in love with Jake.'

Jaz laughed. 'No, I'm not. I'm not that much of a fool.'

'I think he's in love with you.'

Jaz frowned. 'What makes you think that?'

'He bought you that ring for one thing,' Miranda said. 'Look at it. It's the most beautiful ring I've ever seen—apart from my own, of course.'

'It's just a prop.'

'A jolly expensive one.' Miranda leaned over the counter and lifted the scarf Jaz had tied around her neck. 'Aha! I knew it. More diamonds. That brother of mine has got it *so* bad.'

'It's a goodwill gesture,' Jaz said. 'I helped him nail an important business deal last night.'

Miranda stood back with a grin. 'Has he sent you flowers?'

Just then the bell at the back of the door pinged and in came a deliveryman with an armful of long-stemmed snow-white roses tied with a black satin ribbon. 'Delivery for Miss Jasmine Connolly.'

'I'll take that as a yes,' Miranda said once the deliveryman had left.

'They might be from Myles,' Jaz said. Not that Myles had ever bought flowers in the past. He thought they were a waste of money—ironic, given he had more money than most people ever dreamed of having.

'Read the card.'

Jaz gave her a brooding look as she unpinned the velum envelope from the arrangement. She took out the card and read the message: *I'm sorry. Jake.*

'They're from Jake, aren't they?' Miranda said.

'Yes, but—'

Miranda snatched the card out of Jaz's hand. 'Oh, how sweet! He's saying sorry. Gosh, only a man in love does that.'

'Or a man in the wrong.'

Miranda's smooth brow furrowed in a frown. 'What did he do?'

Jaz shifted her lips from side to side. Why was everything suddenly so darn complicated? 'Haven't you got heaps of dusty old paintings to restore?' she said.

Miranda chewed at her lower lip. 'Is it about that night? I know that's always been a sore point between you two. Is that what he was apologising for?'

Jaz let out a long breath. 'In a way.'

'But he didn't do anything. He didn't sleep with you. He's always flatly denied it. He would never have done anything like that. He thought you were just a kid.' Miranda swallowed. 'He didn't sleep with you…did he?'

'No, but someone else tried to,' Jaz said.

Miranda's eyes went wide in horror. 'What do you mean?'

'I stupidly flirted with this guy at the party after I left Jake's room,' Jaz explained. 'I only did it as a payback to Jake. I don't know how it happened but I suddenly found myself fighting off this drunken guy in one of the downstairs bathrooms. I thought he was going to rape me. I was so shocked and frightened but somehow I managed to get away.'

Miranda's hands were clasped against her mouth in shock. 'Oh, my God! That's awful! Why didn't you tell me?'

'I wanted to tell you,' Jaz said. 'Many times. But I just couldn't bring myself to do it. You were dealing with Mark's cancer and I didn't want to add to your misery. I felt so ashamed and dirty.'

'Oh, you poor darling,' Miranda said, flinging her arms around Jaz and hugging her. 'I wish I'd known so I could have done something to help you. I feel like I've let you down.'

'You didn't,' Jaz said. 'You've always been there for me.'

Miranda pulled back to look at her. 'So that's why you only ever dated vanilla men, isn't it?'

She scrunched up her nose. 'What do you mean?'

'You know exactly what I mean,' Miranda said. 'Bland men. Men you can control. You've never gone for the alpha type.'

Jaz gave a little lip shrug. 'Maybe…'

Miranda was still looking at her thoughtfully. 'So Jake was the first person you've ever told?'

Jaz nodded. 'Weird, huh?'

'Not so weird,' Miranda said. 'You respect him. You always have. That's why he annoys you so much. He sees the you no one else sees.'

Jaz fingered the velvet-soft petals of the roses once Miranda had left. Why had Jake sent her white roses? They were a symbol of purity, virtue and innocence. Was that how he saw her?

Miranda was full of romantic notions because

she was madly in love herself. Of course she would like to think her brother was in love with her best friend. But Jake wasn't the type to fall in love. He was too much of a free agent.

Not that Jaz had any right to be thinking along those lines. She was on a mission to win back Myles. Myles was the man she planned to settle down with. Not a man like Jake who would pull against the restraints of commitment like a wild stallion on a leading rein.

Myles was safe and predictable.

Jake was danger personified.

But that didn't mean she couldn't flirt with danger just a wee bit longer.

Jake had never been so fed up with work. He couldn't get his mind to focus on the spreadsheets he was supposed to be analysing. All he wanted to do was go to Jaz's boutique and see if she was still speaking to him. She hadn't called or texted since they had parted last night. The absence of communication would have delighted him a week ago. Now it was like a dragging ache inside his chest. She was a stubborn little thing. She would get on her high horse and not come down even if it collapsed beneath her. That was why she was still hung up on Myles. She wasn't in love with her ex. It was her pride that had taken a hit. She hadn't even told the guy the most devastating thing that had happened to her.

Jake couldn't think about that night without feeling sick. He blamed himself. He had brought that on her by being so insensitive. Why hadn't he gone and checked on her later? He could at least have made an effort to see she was okay. But no, he had partied on as if nothing was wrong, leaving her open to exploitation at the hands of some lowlife creep who had tried to take advantage of her in the worst way imaginable.

Jake's phone buzzed with an incoming message. He picked it up to read it:

Thanks for the roses. Jaz.

He smiled and texted back:

Free for dinner tonight?

Her message came back:

Busy.

He frowned, his gut tensing when he thought of whom she might be busy with. Was it Myles? Was she meeting her ex to try and convince him to come back to her? He waited a minute or two before texting back:

We still on for the w/end?

She texted back.

If u r free?

Jake grimaced as he thought of wandering around a wedding expo all weekend but he figured a man had to do what a man had to do.

He texted back.

I'm all yours.

CHAPTER EIGHT

JAZ WAS READY and waiting for Jake to come to her flat on Friday after work to pick her up. They had only communicated via text messages since yesterday. He had called a couple of times but she hadn't answered or returned the calls. Not that he had left a voice mail message. She hadn't realised how much she had been looking forward to hearing his voice until she checked her voice mail and found it annoyingly silent. Myles, on the other hand, had left several messages asking to meet with her to talk. They were each a variation on his earlier call where he'd told her Jake would never stick around long enough to cast a shadow.

The funny thing was Jake had cast a very long shadow. It was cast all over her life. She could barely recall a time when he hadn't been in it. Ever since she was eight years old she had been a part of his life and he of hers. Even once their charade was over he would still be a part of her life. There would be no avoiding him, not with Julius and Holly's wedding coming up, not to mention Miranda and Leandro's a few months after. Jaz was going to be a bridesmaid at both. There would be other family gatherings to navigate: Christmas, Easter and birthdays. His mother Elisabetta was turning sixty next month in late November and there was no way either Jake or Jaz could ever do a no-show without causing hurt and the sort of drama everyone could do without.

The doorbell sounded and her heart gave a little flutter. Jake was fifteen minutes early. Did that mean he was looking forward to the weekend? Looking forward to being with her? She opened the door to find Myles standing there with a sheepish look on his face. 'Myles…' Jaz faltered. 'Erm…I'm kind of busy right now.'

'I have to talk to you,' he said. 'It's important you hear it from me before you hear it from someone else.'

'Hear what?'

'I'm seeing someone else. It's…serious.'

Jaz blinked. 'How serious?'

'I know it seems sudden but I've known her for ages. We were childhood friends. Do you re-member me telling you about Sally Coombes?'

'Yes, but—'

'I wasn't unfaithful to you, if that's what you're thinking,' Myles said. 'Not while we were of-ficially together.'

Jaz hadn't been thinking it, which was kind of weird, as she knew she probably should have been. All she could think was that she had to get rid of Myles before Jake got here, as she didn't want Jake to end their 'engagement' before she attended the wedding expo. She couldn't bear

to go to it alone. Everyone would be taking photos and posting messages about her being so
unlucky in love. Not a good look for a wedding
designer. What would that do to her credibility?
To her pride? People would find out eventually.
She couldn't hope to keep Jake acting as her fiancé indefinitely. But one weekend—maybe another couple of weeks—was surely not too much
to ask? 'But you've been calling and leaving all
those messages,' she said. 'Why didn't you say
something then?'

'I wanted to tell you in person,' Myles said.
'I'm sorry if I've hurt you, Jaz. But I've had my
doubts about us for a while now. I guess that's
why I instigated the break. It was only when I
caught up with Sally I realised why I was baulk-
ing. As soon as we started talking, I realised she
was the one. We dated when we were younger.
She was my first girlfriend and I was her first
boyfriend. It's like it's meant to be. I hope you

can understand and find it in yourself to forgive me for messing you around.'

'I don't know what to say…' Jaz said. 'Congratulations?'

Myles looked a little pained. 'I want you to be happy. I really do. You're a great girl. I care about you. That's why I'm so concerned about your involvement with Jake Ravensdale. I don't want him to break your heart.'

Jaz stretched her lips into a rictus smile. 'I'm a big girl. I can handle Jake.'

Myles looked doubtful. 'Sally and I aren't making a formal announcement for a week or two. We thought it would be more appropriate to wait for a bit. I just wanted you to be one of the first to know.'

'Thanks for dropping by,' Jaz said. 'I appreciate it. Now, I'm sure you have heaps to do. I won't keep you. Say hi to Sally for me. Tell her if she wants a good deal on a wedding dress I'm the person she needs to see.'

'No hard feelings?' Myles said.

'No hard feelings,' Jaz said, and was surprised and more than a little shocked to find it was true.

Myles had not long disappeared around the corner when Jake's sports car prowled to the kerb. Jaz watched as he unfolded himself from behind the wheel with athletic grace. He was wearing dark-blue jeans and a round-neck white T-shirt with a charcoal-grey cashmere sweater over the top. His hair was still damp from a recent shower as she could see the deep grooves where either his fingers or a wide-toothed comb had been. His jaw was freshly shaven and as he came up to where she was standing on the doorstep she could smell the clean, sharp citrus tang of his aftershave.

Funny, but she hadn't even noticed what Myles had been wearing, the scent of his aftershave or even if he had been wearing any.

'Am I late?' Jake asked with the hint of a frown between his brows.

'No,' Jaz said. 'Perfect timing.'

He leaned down to press a light-as-air kiss to her mouth. 'That's for the neighbours.' Then he put his arms around her and pulled her close. 'And this one's for me.'

Jaz closed her eyes as his lips met hers in a drugging kiss that made her toes curl in her shoes. His tongue mated with hers in a sexy tangle that mimicked the driving need rushing through her body, and his, if the hard ridge of his erection was any indication.

Her hands went around his waist and her pelvis jammed against the temptation of his, her heart skipping all over the place as he made a deep, growly sound of male pleasure as she gave herself up to the kiss. His hands pressed against her bottom to pull her closer, his touch so intimate, so possessive, she could feel her body preparing itself for him. The ache of need pulsed between her legs, her thighs tingling with nerves activated by the anticipation of pleasure.

Only the fact they were on a busy public street was enough to break the spell as a car went past tooting its horn.

Jake released her with a teasing smile. 'Nice to know you've missed me.'

Jaz gave a dismissive shrug. 'You're a good kisser. But then, you've had plenty of practice.'

'Ah, but there are kisses and there are kisses. And yours, baby girl, are right up there.'

Don't fall for his charm. Don't fall for him, she thought as she followed him to the car.

The drive to Gloucester took just over two hours but the time passed easily with Jake's superb driving and easy conversation. He told her about Bruce Parnell, who was so impressed with Jake's choice of fiancée he had recommended several other big-name clients. 'It's the sort of windfall I'd been hanging out for,' he said. 'Word travels fast in the corporate sector.'

'What are you going to say to him when we're no longer a couple?'

He didn't answer for a moment and when he flashed her a quick smile she noticed it didn't quite make the distance to his eyes. 'I'll think of something.'

It was only as Jaz entered the hotel where the wedding expo was being held that she remembered she had only booked one room. It would look suspicious if she asked for another room or even a twin. She and Jake were supposed to be engaged. Everyone would automatically assume they would share a suite. People had already taken out their camera phones and taken snapshots as they came in. She would look a fool if she asked for separate rooms. What woman in her right mind would pass on the chance to spend the night with Jake Ravensdale? Herself included.

Hadn't she always wanted him? It had been there ever since she'd been old enough to understand sexual attraction. It had gone from a teenage crush to a full-blown adult attraction. It simmered in the air when they were together. How long could she ignore it or pretend it wasn't there? Hadn't she already betrayed herself by responding so enthusiastically to his kiss? Had her overlooking of the hotel reservation been her subconscious telling her what she didn't want to face?

As if Jake sensed her dilemma he leaned down close to her ear and whispered, 'I'll sleep on the sofa.'

Jaz was so distracted by the sensation of his warm breath tickling the sensitive skin around her ear she didn't hear the attendant call her to the counter. Jake put a gentle hand at her back and pressed her forward. She painted a smile on her face and said, 'I have a booking for Connolly.'

'Welcome, Miss Connolly,' the attendant said.

'We have your king deluxe suite all ready for you.'

King deluxe. At least there would be enough room in the bed to put a bank of pillows up as a barricade, Jaz thought as she took the swipe key.

The hotel was going to town on the wedding theme. The suite, on the thirteenth floor, was decked out like a honeymoon suite. French champagne was sitting chilled and frosted in a silver ice bucket with a white satin ribbon tied in a big bow around it. There were two crystal champagne flutes and a cheese-and-fruit plate with chocolate-dipped strawberries on the table. The bed was covered in fresh rose petals and there were heart-shaped chocolates placed on the pillows.

'Hmm,' Jake said, rubbing thoughtfully at his chin. 'No sofa.'

Something in Jaz's belly slipped like a Bentley on black ice. There were two gorgeous wing chairs in the bay window, and a plush velvet-covered love seat, but no sofa. 'Right; well, then, we'll have to use pillows,' she said.

'Pillows?'

'As a barricade.'

He gave a soft laugh. 'Your virtue is safe, sweetheart. I won't touch you.'

Jaz rolled her lips together. Shifted her weight from foot to foot. Knotted her hands in front of her body where they were clutching her tote bag straps. Of course she didn't want to sleep with him. He was her enemy. She didn't even like him... Well, maybe a little. More like a lot. Why the heck didn't he want to sleep with her? She hadn't cracked any mirrors lately. She might not be his usual type but she was female and breathing, wasn't she? Why was he being so fussy all of a sudden? He'd kissed her and she'd felt his reaction to her. He wanted her. She knew it as surely as she knew he was standing there. 'What?' she said. 'You don't find me attractive?'

He frowned. 'Listen, a kiss or two or three is fine, but doing the deed? Not going to happen. Not us.'

'Why not us?'

'You're not my type.'

Jaz bristled. 'I was your type when you kissed me outside my flat. Half of flipping Mayfair was witness to it.'

His frown carved a little deeper. 'You're not serious about taking this to that extreme, are you? This is supposed to be an act. When actors do a love scene they don't actually have sex, you know.'

She moved to the other side of the room to stand in front of the window, folding her arms across her body. 'Fine. I get the message. I'd better tape up all the mirrors. The last thing I need is another seven years of bad luck.'

Jake came up behind her, placed his hands on the tops of her shoulders and gently turned her to face him. He searched her face for endless seconds. 'What about Myles?'

Jaz pressed her lips together and lowered her gaze. 'He's engaged to someone else.'

'God, that was quick.'

'He's known her since childhood. I'm happy for him. I really am. It's just I can't bear the thought of everyone knowing I've been dumped,' she said. 'Especially this weekend.'

His fingers massaged her shoulders. 'What's so important about this weekend?'

Jaz rolled her eyes. 'Duh! Look around you, Jake. This is a winter wedding expo. One of my designs is in the fashion parade tomorrow. Next year I want ten. This is my chance to expand my business. To network and get my name out there.'

'But your personal life should have nothing to do with your talent as a designer.'

'Yes, but you told me on the way down how Mr Parnell looks at you differently now you're—'

she put her fingers up in air-quotation marks '—"engaged". It's the same for me. I design wedding gowns for everyone else but I'm totally rubbish at relationships. What sort of advertising for my brand is that?'

He drew in a breath and dropped his hands from her shoulders, using one hand to push through his hair. 'So…what do you want me to do?'

'Just play along a little longer,' she said. 'I know it's probably killing you but please can you do this one thing for me? Just pretend to be my fiancé until…well, a few more days.'

His brow was furrowed as deep as a trench. 'How many days?'

Jaz blew out an exasperated breath. 'Is it such torture to be tied to me for a week or two? *Is* it? Am I so hideous you can't bear the thought of people thinking you've sunk so low as to do it with—?'

Jake's hands came back to hold her by the

upper arms. 'Stop it. Stop berating yourself like that.'

She looked into his midnight-blue gaze, trying to control her spiralling emotions that were like a twisted knot inside her stomach. 'Do you know what it's like to be the one no one wants?' she said. 'No, of course you don't, because everyone wants you. Even my mother didn't want me. She made that perfectly clear by dumping me on my dad. Not that he wanted me either.'

'Your dad loves you,' Jake said.

Jaz gave him a jaded look. 'Then why did he let me move into the big house instead of staying with him at the gardener's cottage? He was relieved when your parents offered to take me in and pay for my education. He didn't know what to do with an eight-year-old kid. I was an inconvenience he couldn't wait to pass off.'

Jake's expression was clenched so tightly in a frown his eyebrows met over his eyes. 'Did he actually say that to you?'

'He didn't need to,' she said on an expelled breath. 'I'm the one no one wants. It should be tattooed across my forehead—*Unwanted.*'

Jake's hands tightened on her arms. 'That's not true. I want you. I've wanted you for years.'

Jaz moistened her tombstone-dry lips. 'You do? You're not just saying that to make me feel better?'

He brought her close against his body. 'Do you think I could fake that?'

She felt the thickened ridge of him swelling against her body. 'Oh...'

'I've always kept my distance because I don't want the same things you want,' he said. 'I'm not interested in marriage—it's not my gig at all. But a fling is something else. I don't even do those normally. My longest relationship was four days when I was nineteen.'

She pulled at her lower lip with her teeth. 'So you'd agree to a fling with me? Just for a week or two?'

He brushed his thumb over her savaged lip. 'As long as you're absolutely clear on the terms. I'm not going to be that guy waiting at the altar of a church aisle for the bride to show up. I'm the guy working his way through the bridesmaids.'

'I happen to be one of the bridesmaids,' Jaz said. 'At two weddings.'

He gave her a sinful smile as his mouth came down to hers. 'Perfect.'

It was a smouldering kiss with an erotic promise that made Jaz's body quake and shudder with want. Every time his tongue touched hers a dart of lust speared her between the legs. Her body wanted him with a desperation she had never felt with such intensity before. It moved through her flesh in tingling waves, making her aware of her erogenous zones as if it was the first time they had been activated. Her breasts were pressed up against his chest, her nipples already puckered from the friction of his hard body. Her hands fisted in his sweater, holding him in case he changed his mind and pulled back.

His mouth continued its passionate exploration of hers, his tongue making love with hers until she was making whimpering sounds of encouragement and delight.

His light stubble grazed her face as he changed position, his hands splaying through her hair as he held her in an achingly tender embrace. He lifted his mouth off hers, resting his forehead against hers. 'Let's not rush this,' he said.

'I thought you lived in the fast lane?' Jaz said, tracing his top lip with her fingertip.

His expression was gravely serious as he caught her hand and held it in the warmth of his against his chest. 'You deserve more than a quick tumble, Jaz. Way more.'

She looked into the sapphire density of his gaze and felt a fracture form in the carapace around her heart like a fissure running through a glacier. 'Are you worried about what happened in the past? Then don't be. I'm fine with sex. I've had it heaps of times.'

'But do you enjoy it?'

'Of course I do,' she said then added when he gave her a probing look, 'Well, mostly.'

He threaded his fingers through her hair like a parent finger-combing a child's hair. 'Are you sure you want to go through with this? It's fine if you've changed your mind. No man's ever died from having an erection, you know.'

Jaz couldn't help smiling. 'Perhaps not, but I think I might if you don't finish what you started.'

He brought his mouth back down to hers, giving her a lingering kiss that was hot, sexy, sweet and tender at the same time. His hands gently moved over her, skimming her breasts at first before coming back to explore them in exquisite detail. He peeled away her top but left her bra in place, allowing her time to get used to being naked with him. He kissed his way down the slope of her breast, drawing on her nipple through the lace of her bra, which added a whole new dimension of feeling. Then, when he had removed his sweater and shirt, he unhooked her bra and gently cradled her breasts in his hands.

Jaz wasn't generously endowed but the way he held her made her feel as if she could be on a high street billboard advertising lingerie. His thumbs brushed over each of her nipples and the sensitive area surrounding them. He lowered his mouth to her puckered flesh and subjected her to the most delicious assault on her senses. The nerves beneath her skin went into a frenzy of excitement, her blood thrumming with the escalation of her desire.

She ran her hands over his muscled chest, delighting in the lean, hard contours of his body. He hadn't followed the trend of being completely hairless. The masculine roughness of his light chest hair tickled her fingers and then her satin-smooth breasts as he drew her closer. It made her feel more feminine than she had ever felt before.

His hands settled on her hips, holding her against his erection, letting her get the feel of him; not rushing her, not pressuring her. Just holding her. But Jaz's body had urgent needs it wanted assuaged and she moved against him in a silent plea for satiation. She had rarely taken the initiative with a partner before. But with Jake she wanted to express her desire for him, to let him know her body ached to be joined to his.

Jaz went for the waistband of his jeans, un-snapping the metal stud and then sliding down his zip. He sucked in air but let her take control. She traced her fingertips over the tented fabric of his underwear, her belly doing a cart-wheel when she thought of how potent he was, of how gorgeously turned on he was for her, yet controlling it to make her feel safe. She peeled back his underwear, stroking him skin to skin, flicking her gaze up to his to see how he was reacting to her touch. 'You like that?'

'This is getting a little one sided,' he said, pushing her hand away. 'Ladies come first according to my rules.'

'I think I like your rules,' Jaz said as he carried her to the bed as if she weighed no more than one of the feather pillows.

He placed her down amongst the scented rose petals and then, shucking off his jeans but leaving his underwear in place, he joined her. He helped her out of her trousers but left her knickers on. Not that they hid much from his view. Had that been another subconscious thing on her part, to wear her sexiest underwear?

He traced the seam of her body through the gossamer-sheer lace. 'Do you have any idea of how long I've wanted to do this?'

Jaz shivered as his touch triggered her most secret nerves into a leaping dance of expectation. 'Me too,' she said but it was more a gasp of sound as he brought his mouth to her and pressed a kiss to her abdomen just above the line of her knickers.

He slowly peeled the lace down to reveal her womanhood. For once she didn't feel that twinge of shame at being naked and exposed in front of a man. It was like he was worshiping her body, treating it with the utmost respect with every stroke and glide of his hands.

He put his mouth to her, separating her folds so he could pleasure the most sensitive part of all. She had never been entirely comfortable with being pleasured this way. Occasionally she had been tipsy enough to get through it. But this time she didn't need the buffer of alcohol. Nor did she need to pretend. The sensations took her by surprise, every nerve pulling tight before exploding in a cascade of sparks that rippled through her body in pulsating waves.

When it was over she let out a breath of pure

bliss. 'Wow. I think that might've measured on the Richter scale.'

He stroked a hand down the flank of her thigh in a smooth-as-silk caress. 'Want to try for a ten?'

Jaz reached for him, surrounding his taut thickness with her fingers. 'I'd like to see you have some fun first, in the interests of being fair and all.'

He smiled a glinting smile. 'I can't argue with that.'

He reached across her to where he'd left his wallet when he'd removed his jeans and took out a condom, dealing with the business of applying it before he came back to her. He moved over her so she was settled in the cradle of his thighs, one of his legs hitched over her hip so she wasn't taking his whole weight. 'Not too heavy for you?' he said. 'Or would you like to go on top?'

Jaz welcomed the press of his body against

hers, the sexy tangle of their limbs sending a frisson of anticipation through her female flesh. 'No, I like it like this. I don't like feeling like I'm riding a horse.'

He gave a deep chuckle. 'I wouldn't throw you off.'

No, but you'll cast me off when you're ready to move on. Jaz pushed the thought aside and ran her hands up his body from his pelvis to his chest and back again. This was for now. A fling she'd wanted since she was a teenager. This was her chance to have what she had always wanted from him: his sole attention, his searing touch, his mind-blowing caresses, and his gorgeously hot body. She knew and understood the rules. There were no promises being made. There was no hope of 'happy ever after'. It was a mutual lust fest to settle the ache of longing that had started so long ago and had never been sated. It was a way—she rationalised it—to rewrite that night seven years ago. This was what she had wanted from Jake way back then—not to be pawed over by some drunk but to be treated with respect, to be pleasured as well as give it. This was the healing she needed to move on with her life, to reclaim her self-respect and her sexual confidence. 'I want you,' she said. 'I don't think I've ever wanted to have sex more than right now.'

He brushed a wayward strand of hair off her face, his dark gaze lustrous with desire. 'I'm pretty turned on myself.'

She stroked him again, watching as his breathing rate increased with every glide of her hand. 'So I can tell.'

He moved her hand so he could access her body, taking his time to caress her until she was swollen and wet. Her need for him was a consuming ache that intensified with every movement of his fingers. She writhed beneath him, restless to feel the ultimate fulfilment, wanting him to possess her so they both experienced the rapture of physical union.

Finally he entered her, but only a short distance, holding back, allowing her to get used to him. His tenderness made her feel strangely emotional. She couldn't imagine him being so tender with his other lovers. She knew it didn't necessarily mean he was falling in love with her. She wasn't that naïve. But it made her feel special all the same. Wasn't this how her teenaged self had imagined it would be? Jake being so tender and thoughtful as he made beautiful, magical love to her?

He thrust a little deeper, his low, deep groan of pleasure making her skin come up in a spray of goose bumps. He began to move, setting a slow rhythm that sent her senses reeling with delight. Each movement of his body within hers caused a delicious friction that triggered all her nerve endings, making them tingle with feeling. She lifted her hips to meet each downward thrust, aching for the release that was just out of reach. Her body was searching for it, every muscle contracting, straining, swelling and quivering with the need to fly free.

He slipped his hand down between their rocking bodies, giving her that little bit of extra coaxing that sent her flying into blessed oblivion. Her body shook with the power of it as each ripple turned into an earthquake. It was like her body had split into thousands of tiny pieces, each one spinning off into the stratosphere. She lost all sense of thought. Her mind had switched off and allowed her body free rein.

He didn't take his own pleasure until hers was over. She held him to her as his whole body tensed before he finally let go, but he did so without any increase in pace, without sound. Had he done that for her sake? Held back? Restrained his response so she hadn't felt overwhelmed or threatened? He hadn't rushed to the end. He hadn't breathed heavily or gripped her too hard, as if he had forgotten she was there.

He didn't roll away but continued to hold her as if he was reluctant to break the intimate union of their bodies.

Or was she deluding herself?

Had he been disappointed? Had she not measured up to his other lovers? She was hardly in the same league. She might have had multiple partners but still nowhere near the number he'd had. Compared to him, she was practically a novice.

One of his hands glided up and down the length of her forearm in a soft caress that made her skin tingle as if champagne bubbles were moving through her blood. 'You were amazing,' he said.

Jaz couldn't ignore the doubts that were winding their way through her mind like a rampant vine. Hadn't she been exciting enough for him? Hadn't her body delighted his the way his had delighted hers? Was that why his response had been so toned down? Maybe he hadn't toned it down. Maybe she hadn't quite 'done it' for him. The chemistry he had talked about hadn't delivered on its promise.

It was *her* fault. Of course it was. Wasn't that why she had been engaged three times and summarily dumped?

She was rubbish at sex.

Jaz eased out of his embrace, reached for one of the hotel bathrobes and slipped it on, tying the waist ties securely. 'You don't have to lie to me, Jake,' she said. 'I know I'm not crash-hot in bed. There's no point pretending I am.'

He frowned as if she was speaking Swahili instead of English. 'Why on earth do you think that?'

She folded her arms, shooting him a flinty look. 'It's probably my fault for talking you into it. If you didn't want to do it then you should've said.'

He swung his legs over the edge of the bed and came over to stand in front of her. He was still completely naked while Jaz was wrapped as tightly as an Egyptian mummy. He put one of his hands on her shoulder and used the other to edge up her chin so her eyes meshed with his. 'You didn't talk me into anything, Jaz,' he said. 'I just didn't want you to feel uncomfortable. Not our first time together.'

She rolled her lips together before releasing a little puff of air. 'Oh…'

He gently brushed back her hair, his eyes searching hers for a moment or two. 'Was that night at the party your first experience of kissing and touching?' he finally asked.

Jaz chewed one corner of her mouth. 'I wanted it to be you. That was my stupid teenage fantasy—that you would be the first person to make love to me.'

He gave her a pained look, his eyes dark and sombre with regret. 'I'm sorry.'

She twisted her lips in self-deprecating manner. 'I guess that's why sex has always been a bit awkward for me. I never felt comfortable unless I was in a committed relationship. But even then I often felt I wasn't up to the mark.'

'You have no need to feel inadequate,' he said. 'No need at all.'

She rested her hands on the wall of his naked chest, her lower body gravitating towards his arousal as if of its own volition. 'You said "our first time together". Does that mean there's going to be a second or a third?'

He put a hand in the small of her back and drew her flush against him, his eyes kindling with sensual promise. 'Start counting,' he said and lowered his mouth to hers.

CHAPTER NINE

JAKE HAD NEVER made love with such care and concern for a partner. Not that he'd been unduly rough or selfish with any of his past lovers, but being with Jaz made him realise what he had been missing in his other encounters. The level of intimacy was different, more focused, more concentrated. The slow burn of desire intensified and prolonged the pleasure. Each stroke of her soft hands made his blood pound until he could feel it in every cell of his body. Her lips flowered open beneath his, her tongue tangling with his in an erotic duel that sent a current of electricity through his pelvis. He held her to his hardness, delighting in the feel of her lithe body moulded against his.

He slipped a hand through the V-neck of her

bathrobe to cup her small but perfect breasts; her skin was as smooth as satin, her nipples pert with arousal. He lowered his mouth to her right breast, teasing her areola with his tongue, skating over her tightly budded nipple, before drawing it into his mouth as she gave a breathless moan of approval. He moved to her left breast, taking his time to explore and caress it with the same attention to detail.

He worked his way up from her breasts to linger over the delicate framework of her collarbone, dipping his tongue into the shallow dish below her neck. Her skin was perfumed with grace notes of honeysuckle and lilac with a base note of vanilla. He spread his fingers through her hair, cradling her head as he kissed her deeply. Her soft little sounds of longing made his heart race and his blood run at fever pitch. Her tongue danced with his in flicks, darts and sweeps that made him draw her even closer to his body.

He eased her bathrobe off her shoulders, letting it fall in a puddle at her feet. He slid his hands down her body to grasp her by the hips, letting her feel the fullness of his erection against her mound. She moved against him, silently urging him on. He left her only long enough to get another condom, quickly applying it before he led her back to the bed. She held her arms out to him as he joined her on the mattress, wrapping them around his neck as he brought his mouth back down to hers.

When he entered her tight, wet heat he felt every ripple of her body welcoming him, massaging him, thrilling him. He began to move in slow thrusts, each one going deeper than the first, letting her catch his rhythm. She whimpered against his mouth, soft little cries of need that made the hairs on his scalp tingle. He continued to rock against her, with her, each movement of their bodies building to a crescendo. He could feel the build-up of tension in her body, the way she strained, gasped and urged him on by gripping his shoulders, as if anchoring herself.

He reached down to touch her intimately, stroking her slick wetness, feeling her swell and bud under his touch, the musky scent of her arousal intermingled with his, intoxicating his senses like the shot of an illicit drug. Her orgasm was so powerful he could feel it contracting against his length, triggering his own release until he was flying as high and free as she.

This time he didn't hold back. He couldn't. He gave a deep groan and pumped and spilled. The rush of pleasure swept through him, spinning him away from everything but what was happening in his body.

Jake had never been big on pillow talk or cuddling in the afterglow. He'd never been good at closeness and contact once the deed had been done.

But with Jaz it was different.

He felt different.

He wasn't sure why. Maybe it was because she wasn't just another girl he had picked up hardly long enough to catch her name. She was someone he knew. Had known for years. She was someone who mattered to him. She was a part of his life—always had been and probably always would be.

He felt protective of her, especially knowing his role in what had happened to her. He wanted her to feel safe and respected. To be an equal partner in sex, not a vessel to be used and cast aside.

But isn't that what you usually do? Use them and lose them?

The thought came from the back of his conscience like a lone heckler pushing through a crowd.

He used women, yes, but they used him back. They knew the rules and played by them. If he thought a woman wasn't going to stick to the

programme, he wouldn't allow things to prog-
ress past a drink and a flirty chat. He was a dab
hand at picking the picket-fence-and-puppies
type. But the women that pursued him were
mostly out for a good time, not a long time,
which suited him perfectly.

He didn't want the responsibility of a relationship. He found the notion of a committed
relationship suffocating. Having to answer to
someone, having to take care of their emotional
needs, being blamed when things didn't work
out, seemed to him to nothing short of torture.
He didn't need that sort of drama. He had seen
enough during his childhood. Watching his parents fight and tear each other down only to make
up as if nothing was wrong had deeply unsettled
him. He never knew what was real, what was
dependable and what wasn't. Life with his parents had been so unpredictable and tempestuous
he had decided the only way he could tolerate
a connection with someone would be to keep it

focused solely on the physical. Emotion had no place in his flings with women.

But for some reason it felt right to hold Jaz in his arms: to idly stroke his fingers up and down her silky skin, her slender back, her neat bottom, her slim thighs. He liked the feel of her lying up against him, her legs still entangled with his. He liked the soft waft of her breath tickling the skin against his neck where her head was buried against him.

He liked the thought that she trusted him enough to share her body with him without fear or shame.

Or maybe it was a pathetic attempt on his part to right the wrongs of the past. To absolve himself from the yoke of guilt about what had happened to her.

As if that's ever going to happen.

Jaz lifted her head out from against his neck and shoulder to look at him. 'Thank you,' she said softly.

Jake tucked a strand of her hair back behind her ear. 'For what? Giving you a ten on the Richter scale?'

'It was a twelve,' she said with a crooked little smile, then added, 'But no. For being so… considerate.'

He picked up one of her hands and kissed the ends of her fingers. 'I'm not sure anyone I know would ever describe me as considerate.'

'You like people to think you're selfish and shallow but deep down I know you're not. You're actually really sensitive. The rest is all an act. A ruse. A defence mechanism.'

He released her hand as he moved away to get off the bed. He shrugged on the other fluffy bathrobe, watching as her teeth started pulling at her lower lip as if she sensed what was coming. *Good*, he thought. *Because I'm not going to pull any punches*. There was no way he was going to play at happy families. No way. Sure, the sex was good. Better than good, when it came to that. But that was all it was: sex. If she was starting to envisage him dressed in a tux standing at the end of the aisle then she had better think again. *Freaking hell.* Next she would be talking about kids and kindergarten bookings.

'Here's what a selfish bastard I am, Jasmine,' he said. 'If you don't stop doing that doe-eyed thing to me, I'm going to head back to London and leave you to face that bunch of wedding-obsessed wackos downstairs all on your own.'

She sat up and pulled the sheet up, hugging her knees close to her chest, her misty eyes entreating. 'Please don't leave… This weekend is important to me. I have everything riding on it. I don't want anything to go wrong.'

He wanted to leave. Bolting when things got serious was his way of dealing with things. But there was young Emma Madden to consider. If Jaz took it upon herself to let that particular cat out of the bag as payback if he left then he could say goodbye to his business deal. Bruce Parnell would withdraw from the contract for sure. That sort of mud had a habit of sticking and making a hell of a mess while it did. Jake's reputation would be shot. He wouldn't be seen in the public eye as just a fun-loving playboy. He would be seen as a lecherous cradle snatcher with all its ghastly connotations.

'I signed up for two weeks.' He held up two fingers for emphasis. 'That's all. After that, we go our separate ways. Those are the rules.'

'Fine,' she said. 'Two weeks is all I want from you.'

He sent her a narrow look. 'Is it?'

Her expression was cool and composed but he noticed how her teeth kept pulling at her lip. 'I'm not falling in love with you, Jake. I was merely making an observation about your character. Your prickliness proves my point. You don't like people seeing your softer, more sensitive side.'

What softer side? She had romantic goggles on. A couple of good orgasms and she was seeing him as some sort of white knight. 'Don't confuse good physical chemistry with anything else, okay? I'm not interested in anything else. And nor should you be until you've sorted out why you keep attracting the sort of guys who won't stick around long enough to put a ring on your finger and keep it there.'

She gave him a pert look. 'Maybe you could tell me what I'm doing wrong, since you're the big relationships expert.'

Jake watched as she took her sweet ass time getting off the bed to slip on a bathrobe. She didn't bother doing up the waist ties but left the sides hanging open, leaving her beautiful body partially on show. For some reason it was more titillating than if she had been standing there stark naked. His blood headed south until he was painfully erect.

Everything about her turned him on. The way she moved like a sleek and graceful cat. The way she tossed her hair back behind her shoulders like some haughty aristocrat. The way she looked at him with artic eyes while her body radiated such sensual heat. It was good to see her act more confident sexually but he couldn't help feeling she was driving home a point. But he was beyond fighting her over it. He wanted her and he only had two weeks to make the most of it. 'What time do you have to be downstairs?' he asked.

She pushed back her left sleeve to check the watch on her slender wrist. It was one his parents had bought for her for her twenty-first birthday. Another reminder of how entwined with his life she was and always would be. 'An hour,' she said. 'I have to check my dress is properly steamed and pressed for the fashion parade tomorrow.'

He held out his hand. 'Have a shower with me.'

She looked at his hand. Returned her gaze to his with a little flicker of defiance in hers. 'Won't you be quicker on your own?'

'Yeah, but it won't be half as much fun.'

CHAPTER TEN

JAZ'S BODY WAS still tingling when she went downstairs with Jake for the welcome-to-the-expo drinks party. He kept giving her smouldering glances as they mingled amongst the other designers and expo staff. She wondered if people knew what they had been up to in the shower only minutes earlier. She had hardly had time to get her hair dry and put on some make-up after he had pleasured every inch of her body.

Of course people knew. He was Jake Ravensdale. What he didn't know about sex wasn't worth knowing. Wasn't her thrumming body proof of that? He only had to look at her with that dark-as-midnight gaze and her inner core would leap in excitement. She saw the effect he had on every woman in the room. Hers wasn't the only pulse racing, the only breath catching in her throat, the only mind conjuring up what she would like to do with him when she got him alone.

Congratulations came thick and fast from the people Jaz knew, as well as many she didn't. It made her feel a little less conflicted about continuing the charade. It was only for two weeks. Two weeks to enjoy the sensual magnificence of a man she had hated for years.

Just shows how easy it is to separate emotion from sex.

One of the models came over with a glass of champagne in one hand. 'Hi, Jake, remember me? We met at a company party last year.'

Jake gave one of his charming smiles. 'Sure I do. How are you?'

The young woman gave a little pout. 'I was fine until I heard you got yourself engaged. No one saw *that* coming.'

Jaz was getting a little tired of being ignored like she was a piece of furniture. 'Hi,' she said holding out her hand to the model. 'I'm Jake's fiancée, Jasmine Connolly. And you are…?'

'Saskiaa with two "a"s,' the girl said with a smile that lasted only as long as her handshake. 'When's the big day?'

'December,' Jaz said. 'Boxing Day, actually.' Why shouldn't she make Jake squirm a bit while she had the chance? 'We're hoping for a white wedding in every sense of the word.'

Jake waited until the model had moved on before he leaned down close to Jaz's ear. 'Boxing Day?'

Jaz looked up at him with a winsome smile. 'I quite fancy the idea of a Christmas wedding. The family will already be gathered so it would be awfully convenient for everyone, don't you think?'

He smiled but it got only as far as his mouth, and that was probably only for the benefit of others who were looking at them. 'Don't overplay it,' he said in an undertone only she could hear.

Jaz kept her smile in place. 'You didn't re-member that girl, did you?'

A frown pulled at his brow. 'Why's that an issue for you?'

'It's not,' she said. 'I don't expect you even ask their name before you sleep with them.'

'I ask their permission, which is far more im-portant in my opinion.'

Jaz held his look for as long as she dared. 'I know it comes as naturally to you as breathing, but I would greatly appreciate it if you wouldn't flirt with any of the women, in particular the models. Half of them look as if they should still be in school.'

His mouth curved upward in a sardonic smile. 'My parents would be enormously proud of you. You're doing a perfect jealous fiancée imper-sonation.'

She snatched a glass of champagne off a pass-ing waiter for something to do with her hands. 'Don't screw this up for me, Jake,' she said through tight lips in case anyone nearby could lip-read. 'I need to secure the booking for next year's expo. Once that's in the bag, you can go back to your "single and loving it" life.'

He trailed a lazy fingertip down her arm from the top of her bare shoulder to her wrist. 'Just wait until I get you alone.'

Jaz shivered as his eyes challenged hers in a sexy duel. His touch was like a match to her tinderbox senses. Every nerve was screaming for more. 'Now who's overplaying it?'

He slipped a hand to the nape of her neck and drew her closer, bending down to press a lingering kiss on her lips. Even though Jaz's eyes were closed in bliss she could see the bright flashes of cameras going off around them. After a moment he eased back and winked at her devilishly. 'Did I tell you how gorgeous you look tonight?'

Jaz knew he was probably only saying it for the benefit of others but a part of her wanted to believe it was true. She placed a hand on the lapel of his suit jacket, smoothing away an imaginary fleck of lint. 'You've scrubbed up pretty well yourself,' she said. 'Even without a tie.'

He screwed up his face. 'I hate the things. They always feel like they're choking me.'

Typical Jake. Hating anything that confined or restrained him. 'I suppose that's why you got all those detentions for breaking the uniform code at that posh school you went to?'

He grinned. 'I still hold the record for the most detentions in one term. Apparently I'm considered a bit of a legend.'

Jaz shook her head at him, following it up with a roll of her eyes. 'Come on.' She looped her arm through his. 'I want to have a look at the displays.'

Oh, joy, Jake thought as Jaz led him to where the wedding finery was displayed in one of the staterooms. The sight of all those meringue-like wedding gowns and voluminous veils was enough to make him break out in hives. Or maybe it was the flowers. There were arrangements of every size and shape: centrepieces, towers of flowers, bouquets, bunches and buttonholes. There were displays of food, wine and French champagne, a honeymoon destination stand and a bespoke jeweller in situ. There were a few men there partnering their fiancées or girlfriends but they were pretty thin on the ground. Jake understood Jaz wanted to secure her signing for next year but he couldn't help feeling she had insisted he accompany her as a punishment.

But that was one of the things he secretly admired in her. She was feisty and stood her ground with him. She was the only woman he knew who didn't simper at him or adapt to suit him. He felt the electric buzz of her will tussling with his every time she locked gazes with him. For years they had done their little stand-off thing. What would they do once they parted company? Would they go back to their old ways or find a new way of relating? With two family weddings coming up, it would be tasteless to be at loggerheads. There was enough of that going around with his parents' carry-on. The dignified thing would be to be mature and civil about it and be friends.

But would he ever be able to look at her as a friend without thinking of how she came apart in his arms? How it felt when he held her close? How her mouth tasted of heat, passion and sweetness mixed in a combustible cocktail that made his senses whirl out of control? Would he ever be able to stand beside her and not want to pull her into his arms?

He'd slept with a lot of women but none of them had had that effect on him. He barely gave his lovers another thought once he moved on to the next. Was it because Jaz was someone who had always been on the periphery of his life?

Sometimes even at the centre, at the very heart, of his family?

Had that familiarity added something to their love-making?

It wasn't just physical sex with her. There were feelings there…feelings he couldn't describe. He cared about her. But then everyone in his family cared about her.

Every time he looked at her he felt the stirring in his groin. He couldn't look at her mouth without thinking of how it felt fused to his own. How her tongue felt as it played with his, how her body felt as she pushed herself, as if she wanted to crawl into his skin and never leave. Even now with her arm looped through his he could feel the brush of her beautiful body against his side. He couldn't wait to get her back to their suite and get her naked.

They walked past a photographer's stand but then Jaz suddenly swivelled and, pulling Jake by the hand, led him back to where the photographer had set up a romantic set with love-hearts, red roses and a velvet-covered sofa in the shape of a pair of lips. 'Can you take our picture?' she asked the photographer.

'Sure,' the photographer said. 'Just sit together on the sofa there for a sec while I frame the shot.'

Jake looked down at Jaz sitting snuggled up by his side as if butter wouldn't melt in her hot little mouth. 'I'm keeping a score,' he said in an undertone. 'Just thought I'd put that out there.'

She gave him a sly smile. 'So am I.'

Jaz thought she might have overdone it with the champagne, or maybe it was being with Jake all evening. Being with him made her tipsy, giddy with excitement. He never left her side; his arm was either around her waist or he held hands with her as she worked the room. It was a torturously slow form of foreplay. Every look, every touch, every brush of his body against hers was a prelude to what was to come. She could see the intention in his dark-blue gaze. It was blatantly, spine-tinglingy sexual. It made every inch of her flesh shiver behind the shield of her clothes, every cell of her body contracting in feverish anticipation.

'Time for bed?' Jake said, his fingers warm and firm around hers.

Jaz felt something in her belly slip sideways. When he touched her like that she couldn't stop thinking of where else he was going to touch her when he got her alone. Her entire body tingled in anticipation. Even the hairs on the nape of her neck shivered at the roots. 'I wonder if we'll win the "most loved-up couple" photo competition?' she said. 'Or the all-expenses-paid wedding and honeymoon package? That would be awesome.'

His eyes sent her a teasing warning. 'Don't push it, baby girl.'

She laughed as he led her to the lift. 'I can't remember a time when I've enjoyed myself more. You should have seen your face when that florist threw you that bouquet. You looked like you'd caught a detonated bomb.'

The lift doors sprang open and Jake pulled her in, barely waiting long enough for the doors to close to bring his mouth down to hers in a scorching kiss. Jaz linked her arms around his neck, pressing as close to him as she could to feel the hardened length of him against her tingling pelvis. He put a hand on one of her thighs and hooked it over his hip, bringing her into closer contact with the heat and potency of him. She could see out of the corner of her eye their reflection in the mirrored walls. It was shockingly arousing to see the way their bodies strained to be together, the flush on both of their faces as desire rode hard and fast in their blood.

Jake put his hand on the stop button and the lift came to a halt. Jaz looked at the erotic intent in his eyes and a wave of lust coursed through her so forcefully she thought she would come on the spot. He nudged her knickers to one side while she unzipped his trousers with fingers that shook with excitement. How he got a condom on so quickly was a testament to how adept he was at sex, she thought. He entered her with a slick, deep thrust that made her head bang against the wall of the elevator. He checked himself at her gasp, asking, 'Are you okay?'

Jaz was almost beyond speech, her breath coming out in fractured, pleading bursts. 'Yes… oh, yes… Don't stop. *Please* don't stop.'

He started moving again, each thrust making her wild with need. He put one of his hands on the wall beside her head to anchor himself as he drove into her with a frantic urgency that made the blood spin, sizzle and sing in her veins. He brought his hand down between their joined bodies, his fingers expertly caressing her until her senses exploded. She clung to him as the storm broke in her, through her, over her.

He followed close behind, three or four hard

pumps; a couple of deep, primal grunts and it was over.

Jaz wriggled her knickers back in place and smoothed her dress down as the lift continued up to their floor. 'I reckon you must hold some sort of record for getting a condom on,' she said into the silence. 'It's like a sleight of hand thing. Amazing.'

He gave her a glinting look as he zipped his trousers. 'Always pays to be prepared.'

A shiver danced its way down her spine as he escorted her out of the lift to their suite, his hand resting in the small of her back. Once they were inside their suite he closed the door and pulled her to him until she was in the circle of his arms. 'Happy with how tonight went?' he said.

Was he talking about her business or their love-making? 'I've got a meeting with the expo organisers next week,' Jaz said. 'It's an exciting opportunity. I'm hoping it will lead to bigger events, maybe even internationally.'

He smoothed a wisp of her hair back off her face. 'Why did you choose to design wedding gear? Why not evening, or fashion in general?'

Jaz slipped out of his hold, feeling a lecture coming on. Of course he would think weddings were a waste of time and money. He was a playboy. A wedding was the last thing on earth that would interest him. But to her they signified everything she had dreamed about as a child. Her parents hadn't married. They hadn't even made a formal commitment to each other. They had just hooked up one night and look how that had turned out. She had been passed between them like a parcel no one wanted until finally her mother had dumped her with her dad without even saying goodbye or 'see you later'.

'Jaz?'

She turned to look at him, her mouth set. 'Do you know what it's like to grow up without a sense of family? To have to *borrow* someone else's family in order to feel normal?'

Jake frowned. 'I'm not sure what that has to do with your choice of career but—'

'It has *everything* to do with it,' Jaz said. 'For as long as I can remember, I wanted to be normal. To have normal parents, not one who's off her face most of the time and the other who hadn't wanted a kid in the first place. I didn't have anything from either of my parents that made me feel a part of a unit. I was a mistake, an accident, an inconvenience.' She folded her arms and continued. 'But when a couple marries, it's different. It's a public declaration of love and commitment and mostly—not always, but mostly—one expressing a desire to have children.'

Jaz looked at him as the silence swelled. Had she said too much? Revealed too much? What did it matter? She was tired of him criticising her choices. 'A wedding dress is something most brides keep for the rest of their lives,' she said. 'It can be passed down from a mother to a daughter. General fashion isn't the same. It's seasonal, transient. Some pieces might be passed on but they don't have the emotional resonance a wedding dress has. That's why I design wedding gowns. Every woman deserves to be a princess for a day. I like being able to make that wish come true.' *Even if I can't make it come true for myself.*

Jake gave a slow nod. 'Sounds reasonable.'

'But you think I'm crazy.'

'I didn't say that.'

Jaz went to the drinks fridge and poured a glass of mineral water, taking a sip before she turned to face him again. He was looking at her with a contemplative look on his face, his brows drawn together, his mouth set in a serious line, his gaze centred on hers. 'I'm sorry if tonight's been absolute torture for you but this weekend's really important to me.'

His mouth tilted in a wry smile. 'You're not

one bit sorry. You've enjoyed every minute, watching me squirm down there.'

Jaz smiled back. 'It was rather fun, I have to admit. I can't wait to see what press photos show up. I wonder if they got the one of you with the bouquet. Or maybe I should text it or post it online?'

He closed the distance between them and pulled her down to the bed in a tangle of limbs. 'Cheeky minx,' he said, eyes twinkling with amusement.

Jaz stroked the sexy stubble on his face, her belly fluttering with excitement as his hard body pressed against hers. His hooded gaze went to her mouth, his thumb coming up to brush over her lower lip until it tingled, as if teased by electrodes. 'What are you thinking?'

'You mean you can't tell?' he said with a wicked sparkle in his eyes.

She snatched in a breath as his body moved against her, triggering a tide of want that flooded her body, pooling hotly in her core. 'When you hook up with someone, how many times do you have sex with them in one night?'

A frown creased his forehead. 'Why do you want to know?'

Jaz traced the trench of his frown with her finger. 'Just wondering.'

He caught her hand and pinned it on the bed beside her head, searching her gaze for a pulsing moment. 'Wondering what?'

'If you've done it more with me than with anyone else.'

'And if I have?'

She looked at his mouth. 'Is it…different…? With me, I mean?'

He nudged up her chin with a blunt fingertip, locking his gaze with hers. 'Different in what way?'

Jaz wasn't sure why she was fishing so hard for compliments. He had made it clear how long their fling was going to last. Just because he had made love to her several times tonight didn't mean anything other than he had a high sex drive. He was, after all, a man in his sexual prime. But their love-making was so different from anything she had experienced with other partners. It was more exciting, more satisfying, more addictive, which was a problem because she couldn't afford to get too used to having him. 'I don't know...more intense?'

He slid his hand along the side of her face to splay his fingers through her hair. It was an achingly tender hold that made Jaz's heart squeeze as if someone had crushed it in a vice. Could it be possible he was coming to care for her? *Really* care for her? Was that why their intimacy was so satisfying? Did their physical connection reflect a much deeper one that had been simmering in the background for years?

But she didn't love him.

Not the slavish way she had as a teenager. She was an adult now. Her feelings for him were mature and sensible. She knew his faults and limitations. She didn't whitewash his personality to make him out to be anything he was not. She was too sensible to hanker after a future with him because he wasn't the future type. He was the 'for now' type.

Falling in love with Jake Ravensdale once had been bad enough. To do it twice would be emotional suicide.

'It is different,' Jake said. 'But that doesn't mean I want it to continue longer than we agreed.'

'I'm not asking for an extension,' Jaz said. 'I can't afford to waste my time having a long-term fling with someone who doesn't want the same things I want. I want to get on with my life and find my soul mate. I want to start a family before I'm thirty.'

His frown hadn't quite gone away but now it was deeper than ever. 'You shouldn't rush into your next relationship. Take your time getting to know them. And what's the big rush on having kids? You're only twenty-three. You've got heaps of time.'

'I don't want to miss out on having kids,' Jaz said. 'I know so many women who've left it too late or circumstances have worked against them. I can't imagine not having a family. It's what I've wanted since I was a little girl.'

He moved away from her and got off the bed, scraping a hand through his hair before dropping it back by his side.

Jaz chewed at her lower lip. 'Did I just kill the mood?'

He turned around with a smile that didn't involve his eyes. 'It's been a long day. I'm going to have a shower and hit the sack. Don't wait up.'

When Jake came out of the bathroom after his shower half an hour later, Jaz wasn't in the bed. In fact, she wasn't in the suite. He frowned as he searched the room, even going so far as to check under the bed. Where the hell was she? He glanced at her bag on the luggage rack. She obviously hadn't checked out of the hotel as her things were still here. Although, come to think of it, he wouldn't put it past her to flounce off, leaving him to pack her things. What was she up to? Their conversation earlier had cut a little close to the bone...for him, that was. Why did she have to carry on about marriage and kids all the time? She was a baby herself. Most twenty-three-year-olds were still out partying and having a good time.

But no, Jaz wanted the white picket fence and a bunch of wailing brats. What would happen to her stellar career as a wedding designer then? She would be doing more juggling than a circus act.

And as to finding her soul mate... Did she really believe such a thing existed? There was no such thing as a perfect partner. She was deluding herself with romantic notions of what her life could be like.

Well, he had news for her. It would be just like everyone else's life—boring and predictable.

Jake called her number but it went straight through to voice mail. He paced about the suite, feeling more and more agitated. The weird thing was he spent hours of his life in hotel rooms, mostly alone. He rarely spent the whole night with anyone. It was less complicated when it came to the 'morning after the night before' routine.

But every time he looked at that bed he thought of how it had felt with Jaz, her arms and legs wrapped around him and her hot little mouth clamped to his. He couldn't stop thinking about the lift either. He probably wouldn't be able to get into one ever again without thinking of taking Jaz up against that mirrored wall. His blood pounded at the memory of it. He had been close to doing it without a condom. He still didn't know how he'd got it on in time. He had been as worked up as a teenager on his first 'sure thing' date.

What was it about Jaz that made him so intensely attracted to her? It wasn't like this with his other flings. Once or twice was usually enough before he was ready for more excitement. But with Jaz he was mad with lust. Crazy with it. Buzzing with it. Making love with her eased it for a heartbeat before he was aching for her again. It had to blow out eventually. It *had* to. He wasn't putting down tent pegs just because the sex was good. Just as well they'd agreed on an end date. Two weeks was pushing it. He didn't take that long for holidays because he always got bored. There was no way this was going to continue indefinitely.

No. Freaking. Way.

Jake threw on some clothes and finger-combed his damp hair on his way to the lift. She had to be in the hotel somewhere. He jabbed at the call button. Why the hell was it so slow? Was some other couple holed up in there, doing it? His gut tightened. Surely Jaz wouldn't pick up someone and…? No. He slammed his foot down on the thought like someone stomping on a noxious spider.

The lift was empty.

So was his stomach as he searched the bar for the glimpse of that gorgeous honey-brown head. He went to the restaurant, and then looked through the foyer, but there was no sign of her anywhere. He hadn't realised until then what had fuelled his heart-stopping panic. It hit him like a felling blow right in the middle of his chest. He couldn't draw breath for a moment. His throat closed. He could feel his thudding pulse right down to his fingertips.

He had dismissed her. Rejected her. What if she had been upset and gone downstairs to God knew what? What if some unscrupulous guy had intercepted her? Shoved her into a back room and done the unthinkable?

The stateroom where the displays were set up was closed with a burly security guard posted outside.

The security guard gave Jake the eye as he tried the doorknob. 'Sorry, buddy,' the guard said with a smirk. 'You'll have to wait till morning to try a dress on.'

Jake wanted to punch him.

He retraced his steps; his growing dread making his skin break out in a clammy sweat until his shirt was sticking to his back like cling-film. Where could she have gone? He couldn't get the image of her trapped in some room—*some locked bathroom*—with an opportunist creep mauling her. He would never be able to live with himself if she got hurt under his watch. She was with him. He was supposed to be her partner. Her 'fiancé'. What sort of fiancé would let her wander off alone to be taken advantage of by some stranger? She was gullible with men. Look at the way she'd got engaged three times. He hadn't liked one of them. They were nice enough men but not one of them was worthy of her.

Jake strode past the restrooms. Could she be in there? Locked inside one of the cubicles with someone? He did a quick whip round and checked that no one was watching before he pushed open the outer door. 'Jaz? Are you in there?' There was no answer so he went in through to where the cubicles were.

A middle-aged woman turned from the basins with her eyes blazing in indignation. 'This is the ladies' room!'

'I—I know,' Jake said, quickly back-pedalling with the woman following him like an army sergeant. 'I'm looking for my…er…fiancée.'

The woman blasted him with a look that was as icy as the wind off the North Sea in winter. 'I've met men like you before. Lurking around female toilets to get your sick thrills. I've a good mind to call security.'

Jake looked at her in open-mouthed shock, which didn't seem to help his cause one little bit, because it looked like he'd been sprung doing exactly what the woman accused him of. 'No, no, no,' he said, trying to placate her as she took out her phone. If she took a snapshot of him in the female restrooms and it went viral he could forget about his reputation and his career. Both would be totally screwed. 'My fiancée is this high...' He put his hand up to demonstrate. 'Really pretty with light-brown hair and grey-blue eyes and—'

'Is there a problem?' The security guard from outside the display room spoke from behind Jake.

Jake rolled his eyes. This was turning into such a freaking farce. And meanwhile Jaz was still missing. He turned to face the guard. 'I'm looking for my fiancée. She's not answering her phone. I thought she might be in the ladies' room.'

The security guard's mouth curled up on one side. 'You seem to have a thing for what belongs to the ladies, don't you, buddy?'

Jake clenched his hands in case he was tempted to use them to knock that sneer off the guard's face. *Time to play the famous card.* 'Look, I'm Jake Ravensdale,' he said. 'I'm—'

'I don't care if you're Jack the bloody Ripper,' the guard said. 'I want you out of here before I call the cops.'

'You can check with Reception,' Jake said. 'Get them to check the bookings. I'm here with Jasmine Connolly, the bridal designer.' *Dear God, had Jaz put him on the booking informa-tion?* he thought in panic as the guard took out his intercom device and called the front desk.

The guard spoke to someone at Reception and then put his device back on his belt, his ex-pression now as nice as pie. 'Nice to meet you,

Mr Ravensdale,' he said. 'Enjoy your stay. Oh, and by the way…' He put on a big, cheesy grin. 'Congratulations.'

Jake went back to the suite with his whole body coiled as tight as a spring. He pushed open the door to see Jaz getting ready for bed. 'Where the bloody hell have you been?' he said. 'I've been scouring the hotel from top to bottom for the last hour looking for you.'

'I went down to check on my dress before the room was locked.'

'Did you not think to leave a note or a send me a text?'

A spark of defiance shone in her grey-blue gaze as it collided with his. 'I assumed you were finished with me for the evening. You told me not to wait up.'

Jake smothered a filthy curse under his breath. 'Do you have any idea of how damned worried I was?'

She looked at him blankly. 'Why would you be worried?'

He pushed his hand back through his hair. 'I was worried, that's all.'

She came over to him to lay a hand on his arm. Her soft fingers warmed his flesh, making every one of his taut muscles unwind and others south of the border tighten. 'Are you okay?'

Was he okay? No. He felt like he would never be okay again. *Ever.* His head was pounding with the mother of all headaches. His heart rate felt like someone had given him an overdose of adrenalin. Two overdoses. His legs were shaking. His guts had turned to gravy. 'I'm fine.' Even to his own ears he knew he sounded unnecessarily curt.

'You don't sound it,' Jaz said, frowning at him in concern. 'Are you unwell? Have you caught food poisoning or something? You look so pale and sweaty and—'

'I almost got myself arrested.'

Her eyes rounded. 'What on earth for?'

'Long story.'

'Tell me what happened, Jake,' she said. 'I need to know, since we're here at this expo together, because it could reflect badly on me.'

Should he tell her it all or just a cut-down version? 'I panicked when you weren't in the suite. I didn't know where you'd gone.'

She began to stroke his arm, her eyes as clear, still and lustrous as a mountain tarn as she looked into his. 'Were you worried I wasn't coming back?'

His hands came down on her shoulders in a grip that was unapologetically possessive. 'I was out of my mind with worry,' he said. 'I tried to check the display room but the security guard gave me a hard time. And then he found me coming out of the ladies' toilets—'

Her brow puckered. 'Why'd you go in there?'

Jake swallowed. 'I was worried someone might have cornered you in there and…' He couldn't even say what he'd thought. It was too sickening to be vocalised.

Her eyes softened. 'Oh, you big goose,' she said. 'I'm a big girl now. I can fend for myself, but thanks anyway.'

He brought her closer so her hips were against his, watching the way her tongue came out to moisten her lips; it made every one of those muscles in his groin go rock-hard. 'I swear to God I've aged a decade in the last hour.'

'Doesn't feel like it to me.'

He pressed her even closer. 'I want you.'

A little light danced like a sprite in her gaze. 'Again?'

He walked her backwards toward the bed, thigh to thigh, hip to hip, need to need. 'How much sleep do you need?' he said as he nibbled at her mouth, their breaths intermingling.

'Seven hours—five in an emergency—otherwise I get ratty.'

Jake helped her out of her clothes with more haste than finesse. 'I can handle ratty.'

She gave a tinkling laugh. 'Don't say I didn't warn you.'

He put his mouth on her naked breast, drawing her tight nipple into his mouth. It was music to his ears to hear her breathless moan of pleasure. It made his blood pump all the more frantically. He pushed her gently down on the bed, shoving pillows, petals and clothes out of the way as he came down beside her. He wanted to go slow but his earlier panic did something to his self-control. He needed to be inside her. He needed to be fused with her, to have her writhing and shuddering as he took her to paradise. He needed to quell this feverish madness racing in his blood. Her body gripped him like a fist as he surged into her velvet heat. The ripples of her inner core massaged him inexorably closer to a mind-blowing lift-off. He held on only long enough to make sure she was with him all the way. When she came around him he gave a part-growl, part-groan as he lost himself to physical bliss…

CHAPTER ELEVEN

JAZ WAS TRYING not to show how nervous she was the next morning but Jake must have sensed it because he kept looking at her with a watchful gaze. She picked at the breakfast he had had delivered to their suite but barely any made it to her mouth.

'At least have a glass of juice,' he said, pushing a glass of freshly squeezed orange juice towards her.

'I think I'm going to be sick.'

He took her hand from across the table and gave it an encouraging squeeze. 'Sweetheart, you're going to knock them for six down there.'

She bit down on her lip, panic and nerves clawing at her insides like razor blades whirled in a blender. 'Who am I fooling? I'm just a gardener's daughter from the wrong side of the tracks. What am I doing here pretending I'm a high street designer?'

'Imposter syndrome,' Jake said, leisurely pouring a cup of brewed coffee. 'That's what all this fuss is about. You don't believe in yourself. You think you've fluked it, that someone is going to come up behind you and tap you on the shoulder and tell you to get the hell out of here because you're not up to standard.'

That was exactly what Jaz was thinking. She had been thinking it most of her life. Being abandoned by her mother had always made her feel as if she wasn't good enough. She tried so hard to be the best she could be so people wouldn't leave her. But invariably they eventually did. Three times she had got engaged and each time it had ended. Her fiancés had ended it, not her. She was ashamed to admit she might well have married each and every one of them if they hadn't pulled the plug first. She was so

terrified of failing, she over-controlled everything: her work, her relationships, her life. Her
business was breaking even...just. But she'd had
a lot of help. If it hadn't been for Jake's parents,
she might never have got to where she was.

How long could she go on doing everything
herself? She was constantly juggling. Sometimes she felt like a circus clown on stilts with
twenty plates in the air. She couldn't remember
the last time she'd taken a holiday. She took her
work everywhere. She had Holly's dress with
her in case there was a spare minute to work on
the embroidery. She hadn't had a chance to draw
a single sketch for Miranda. How long could she
go on like that? Something had to give. She was
going to get an ulcer at this rate. Maybe she already had one.

'You're right,' she said on a sigh. 'Every time
I get myself to a certain place, I make myself
sick worrying it's going to be ripped out from
under me.'

'That's perfectly understandable given what happened with your mother.'

Jaz lowered her gaze as she smoothed out a tiny crease in the tablecloth. 'For years I waited for her to come back. I used to watch from the window whenever a car came up the drive. I would get all excited thinking she was coming back, that she had got herself sorted out and was coming back to take me to the new life she'd always promised me. But it never happened. I haven't heard from her since. I don't even know if she's still alive.'

Jake covered her hand with the warm solidness of his. 'You've made your own new life all by yourself. You didn't need her to come back and screw it up.'

'Not *all* by myself,' Jaz said. 'I'm not sure where I'd be if it hadn't been for your parents.' She waited a beat before adding, 'Do you think you could have a look over my books some time? I'm happy to pay you.'

'Sure, but you don't have to pay me.'

'I insist,' Jaz said. 'Your family has helped me enough. I don't want to be seen as a charity case.'

Jake lightly buttered some toast and handed it to her. 'One mouthful. It'll help to settle your stomach.'

Jaz took the toast and bit, chewed and swallowed but it felt like she was swallowing a cotton ball. 'Do you have it?'

'Have what?'

'Imposter syndrome?'

He smiled crookedly, as if the thought was highly amusing. 'No.'

'I suppose it was a silly question,' she conceded. 'Mr Confidence in all situations and with all people.'

A shadow passed over his features like a hand moving across a beam of light. 'There have been times when I've doubted myself.'

'Like when?'

'At boarding school, especially in my senior year,' he said, frowning slightly as he stirred his coffee. 'I played the class clown card so often I lost sight of who I really was. It wasn't until I left school and went to university that I finally found my feet and became my own person instead of being Julius's badly behaved twin brother.'

Jaz had always seen Jake as a supremely confident person. He seemed to waltz through life with nary a care of what others thought of him. She was the total opposite. Her desperate desire to fit in had made her compromise herself more times than she cared to admit. Weren't her three engagements proof of that? She had wanted to be normal. To belong to someone. To be wanted. 'I guess it must be hard, being an identical twin and all,' she said. 'Everyone is always making comparisons between you and Julius.'

There was a small silence.

'Yeah. We look the same but we're not the

same,' Jake said. 'Julius is much more grounded and focused than I am.'

'I don't know about that,' Jaz said. 'You seem pretty grounded to me. You know what you want and go for it without letting anyone get in your way.'

He was frowning again as if a thought was wandering around in his head and he wasn't quite sure where to park it. 'But I don't stick at stuff,' he finally said. 'Not for the long haul.'

'But you're happy living your life that way, aren't you?'

After another moment of silence he gave her an absent smile. 'Yeah, it works for me. Now, have a bit more toast. It'd be embarrassing if you were to faint just when it's your chance to shine.'

Jaz did a last-minute check with the model for the gown she had prepared for the show. It was the first time any of her work would be worn by a professional model on a catwalk. The advertising she had done in the past had been still shots with models from an agency and a photographer who was a friend of a friend.

But this was different. This was her dream coming to life in front of her. Hundreds, possibly thousands or even millions, would see her design if the images went global. It would be the start of the expansion of her business she had planned since she had left design college.

Why then did she still feel like a fraud?

Because she was a fraud.

A fake.

Not because she didn't know how to design and sew a beautiful wedding gown. But because she wasn't in a committed relationship and the ring she was wearing on her finger was going to be handed back in two weeks' time. She was like the blank-faced models wearing the wedding gowns. They weren't really brides. They were acting a role.

Like *she* was acting a role.

She was pretending to be engaged to Jake when all she wanted was to be engaged to him for real. How had she not realised it until now? Or had she been shying away from it because it was a truth she hadn't wanted to face?

She was in love with Jake.

Hadn't she always been in love with him? As a child she had looked up to him as a fun older brother. He had been the playful twin, the one she could have a laugh with. Then when her female hormones had switched on she had wanted him as a woman wanted a man. But she hadn't been a woman back then—she had been a child. He had respected that and kept his distance. Wasn't that another reason why she loved him? He hadn't exploited her youthful innocence. Yes, he hadn't handled her crush with the greatest sensitivity, but at least he hadn't taken advantage of her.

Jaz was done with acting. Done with pretending. How could she stretch this out another week or two? Jake wasn't in love with her. Didn't their conversation over breakfast confirm it? He was happy with the way his life was a single man. He would go back to that life as soon as their 'engagement' ended.

Jake said she could keep the ring but why would she do that? It was little more than a consolation prize. A parting gift. Every time she looked at it she would be reminded of what she wanted and couldn't have. It might be enormous fun being with Jake. It might be wonderful to be his lover and feel the thrill of his desire and hers for him.

But what was she *doing*?

She was living a lie. That was what she was doing. Fooling people that she was in a real relationship with real hopes and dreams for the future. What future? Two weeks of fantastic, mind-blowing sex and then what? Jake would pull the plug on their relationship just like her three exes had done. She would be abandoned. Rejected. Left hanging. Alone.

Not this time. Not again.

This time she would take control. Do the right thing by herself and set the boundaries. Two weeks more of this and she would want it to be for ever. Good grief! She wanted it to be for ever now. That was how dangerous their fling had become. One night of amazing sex and she was posting the wedding invitations.

It was ridiculous.

She was ridiculous.

Jake wasn't a 'for ever' type of guy. He wanted her but only for as long as it took to burn out their mutual attraction. How long would it take? He had set the limit at two weeks. Most of his relationships didn't last two days. Why should she think *she* was so special? Sure they knew each other. They had a history of sorts. They would always be in each other's lives in some way or another.

It would be best to end it now.

On *her* terms.

Before things got crazy. Crazier...because what was crazier than falling in love with a man just because you couldn't have him? That was what she had done. It was pathological. She was in love with a man who didn't—*couldn't*—love her.

It was time to rewrite the script of her life. No longer would she fall for the wrong men. No longer would she settle for second best... even though there was no way she would ever describe Jake as second best. He was first best. *The* best. The most fabulous man she had ever known—but he wasn't hers.

He wasn't anyone's.

It would break her heart to end their affair. Weird to think she'd thought her heart had been broken by her three failed engagements; none of them, even all of them put together, had made her feel anywhere near as sad as ending her fling with Jake.

It wasn't just the sex. It was the way he made her feel as a person. He valued her. He understood her. He knew her doubts and insecurities. He had taught her to put the dark shadow of the past behind her. He protected her. He made her feel safe. He had helped her heal. His touch, his kisses, his glorious love-making, had made her fully embrace her femininity.

He had given her the gift of self-acceptance, but with that gift had come realisation. The realisation she could no longer pretend to be something she was not. She had to stop hiding behind social norms in order to feel accepted. If she never found love with a man who loved her equally, unreservedly and for ever, then she would be better off alone. Settling for anything less was settling for second best. It was compromising and self-limiting and would only bring further heartbreak in the end.

But it would be hard to be around Jake as just a friend. She would go back to being the gardener's daughter—the little ring-in who didn't really belong in the big house.

The girl who didn't belong to anyone.

Jake watched from the front row beside Jaz as her design came down the catwalk. She had only just got to her seat in time to see her moment in the spotlight. The dress was amazing. He found his mind picturing her wearing it. It had a hand-sewn beaded bodice and a frothy tulle skirt that was just like a princess's dress. The veil was set back from the model's head and flowed out behind her like a floating cloud.

If anyone had told him a week ago he'd be sitting at a wedding expo oohing and aahing at wedding gowns he would have said they were nuts. The atmosphere was electric. The ballroom was abuzz with expectation. The music was up-beat and stirring, hardly bridal or churchy at all.

The applause was thunderous when Jaz's design was announced and continued even after the model had left the catwalk. He clapped as loudly as anyone, probably louder. 'Told you they'd love your work,' he said. 'You'll have orders coming out of your ears after this.'

She looked at him with a tremulous smile. 'You think?'

She still doubted herself. Amazing, he thought. What would it take for her to believe she was as good if not better than any of the other designers here? He tapped her on the end of her retroussé nose. 'Sure of it.'

Jake took her hand while the press did their interviews after the show. He was getting quite used to the role of devoted fiancé. Who said he couldn't act? Maybe some of that Ravensdale talent hadn't skipped a generation after all. Or maybe he was getting used to being part of a couple. There was certainly something to be said about knowing who he was going to sleep with that night—earlier, if he could wangle it. Instead of wondering how the sex would be, he knew for certain it would be fantastic. He had never had a more satisfying lover.

Jaz's body was a constant turn-on as it brushed against his as the crowd jostled them. He drew her closer as a photographer zoomed in on them. Her cheek was against his; the fresh, flowery scent of her made his sinuses tingle. She turned her head and he swooped down and stole a kiss from her soft-as-a-pillow mouth, wishing he could get her alone right here and now.

But instead of continuing the kiss she eased back, giving him a distracted-looking smile. Her hands went back to her lap where she was gripping the programme as if she had plans to shred it.

'You okay?' Jake said.

Her gaze was trained on the next set of models strutting their stuff. 'We need to talk,' she said. 'But not here.'

Here it comes. The talk. The talk where she would say she wanted the whole shebang: the promises of for ever, the kids, the dog and the house. The things he didn't want. Had never wanted. Would never want. Why had he thought she would be any different? He had broken his own rules for what? For a fling that should never have started in the first place.

Might as well get it over with. Once the show was over, he took her by the elbow and led her back to their suite. *Their suite.* How cosy that sounded. Like they were a couple. But they weren't a couple. A couple of idiots, if anything. They had no right to be messing around. *He* had no right. She was a part of his family. By getting involved with her he had jeopardised every single relationship she had with his family. Would everyone treat her differently now they knew she had been his lover? Would they look at her differently? Would he be harangued for the next decade for not doing the right thing by her and leaving her alone?

'I know what you're going to say,' Jake said even before he had closed the door of the suite.

She pressed her lips together for a moment. Turned and put the programme and her bag on the bed, then turned back to him and handed him her engagement ring. 'I think it's best if we end things now,' she said. 'Before we head back to London.'

Jake stared at the ring and then at her. She wanted to end it? *Now?* Before the two weeks were up? That wasn't how 'the talk' usually went. Didn't she want more? Didn't she want them to continue their affair? Wasn't she going to cry, beg and plead with him to fall in love with her and marry her? She looked so composed, so determined, as if she had made up her mind hours ago.

'But I thought you said two weeks?'

'I know but I can't do it any more, Jake,' she

said, putting the ring in the top pocket of his jacket and patting it as if for safekeeping. 'It was fun while it lasted but I want to move on with my life.'

'This seems rather…sudden.'

She stepped back and looked up at him with those beautiful storm, sea and mountain-lake eyes. 'Remember when we talked at breakfast?' she said. 'I've been thinking since…I can't pretend to be someone I'm not. It's not right for me or for you. You're not the settling down type and it was wrong of me to shackle you to me in this stupid game of pretend. I should've just accepted Myles's break-up with dignity instead of doing this crazy charade. It will hurt too many people if we let it continue. It has to stop.'

Jake wanted it to stop. Sure he did. But not yet. Not until he was satisfied his attraction to her had burned itself out. It was nowhere near burning out. It had only just started. They'd been lovers two days. *Two freaking days!* That wasn't long enough. He was only just starting to understand her. To know her. How could she want to end it? They were good together. Brilliant. The best. Why end it when they could have two more weeks, maybe even longer, of fantastic sex?

But how *much* longer?

The thought stood up from a sofa in the back of his mind where it had been lounging and stretched. Started walking toward his conscience…

Jake knew she was right. They had to end it some time. It was just he was usually the one to end flings. He was the one in the control seat. It felt a little weird to be on the receiving end of rejection. 'What about Emma Madden?' he said. 'Aren't you worried she might make a comeback when she hears we've broken up?'

'I think Emma is sensible enough to know you're not the right person for her. It will hurt her more if we tell even more lies.'

'What about Bruce Parnell?' *God, how*

*pathetic was he getting? Using his clients as a
lever to get her to rethink her decision?*

'Tell him the truth,' she said. 'That you're not
in love with me and have no intention of marrying me or anyone.'

The truth always hurt, or so people said. But
it didn't look like it hurt Jaz. She didn't seem to
be the least bit worried he wasn't in love with
her. She hadn't even asked him to declare his
feelings, which was just as well, because they
were stuffed under the cushions on that sofa in
his mind and he wasn't going looking for them
any time soon.

'You're right,' he said. 'Best to end it now before my parents start sending out invitations.'

She bit her lip for a moment. 'Will you tell
them or will I?'

'I'll tell them I pulled the plug,' Jake said.
'That's what they'll think in any case.'

Her forehead puckered in a frown. 'But I don't

want them to be angry with you or anything. I can say I got cold feet.'

'Leave it to me. Do you still want me to have a look over your business?'

'You wouldn't mind?'

'Why would I?' he said with a smile that was harder work than it had any right to be. 'We're friends, aren't we?'

Her smile was a little on the wobbly side but he could see relief in every nuance of her expression. 'Yes. Of course we are.'

It was on the tip of his tongue to ask for one more night but before he could get the words out she had turned and started packing her things. He watched her fold her clothes and pack them neatly into her bag. Every trace of her was being removed from the suite.

'I'm getting a lift back to London with one of the photographers,' she said once she was done. 'I thought it would be easier all round.'

'Is the photographer male?' The question

jumped out before Jake could stop it and it had the big, green-eyed monster written all over it.

His question dangled in the silence for a long beat.

'Yes,' she said. 'But I've known him for years.'

Jaz had known *him* for years and look what had happened, Jake thought with a sickening churning in his gut.

She stepped up on tiptoe to kiss his cheek. 'Goodbye, Jake. See you at Julius's wedding.'

Wedding.

Jake clenched his jaw as the door closed on her exit. That word should be damned well banned.

CHAPTER TWELVE

JAZ WAS WORKING on Miranda's dress a few days later when the bell on the back of her shop door tinkled. She looked up and saw Emma Madden coming in, dressed in her school uniform. 'Hi, Emma,' she said, smiling as she put down the bodice she was sewing freshwater pearls on. 'How lovely to see you. How are you?'

Emma savaged her bottom lip with her teeth. 'Is it because of me?'

Jaz frowned. 'Is what because of you?'

'Your break-up with Jake,' she said. 'It's because of me, isn't it? I made such a stupid nuisance of myself and now you've broken up and it's all my fault.'

Jaz came out from behind the work counter and took the young girl's hands in hers. 'Nothing's your fault, sweetie. Jake and I decided we weren't ready to settle down. We've gone back to being friends.'

Emma's big, soulful eyes were misty. 'But you're so perfect for each other. I can't bear the thought of him having anyone else. You bring out the best in him. My stepdad says so too.'

Jaz gave Emma's hands a little squeeze before she released them. 'It's sweet of you to say so but some things are not meant to be.'

'But aren't you...*devastated*?' Emma asked, scrunching up her face in a frown.

Jaz didn't want to distress the girl unnecessarily. No point telling Emma she cried every night when she got into her cold bed. *On. Her. Own.* No point saying how she couldn't get into a lift without her insides quivering in erotic memory. No point saying how every time she ate a piece of toast or drank orange juice she thought of Jake helping her through her fashion show nerves at the expo. 'I'm fine about it,' she said. 'Really. It's for the best.'

Emma sighed and then started looking at the dresses on display. She touched one reverently. 'Did you really make this from scratch?'

'Yup,' Jaz said. 'What do you think? Not too OTT?'

'No, it's beautiful,' Emma said. 'I would love to be able to design stuff like this.'

'Have you ever done any sewing?'

'I did some cross-stitch at school but I'd love to be able to make my own clothes,' Emma said. 'I sometimes get ideas for stuff… Does that happen to you?'

'All the time,' Jaz said. 'See that dress over there with the hoop skirt? I got the idea from the garden at Ravensdene. There's this gorgeous old weeping birch down there that looks exactly like a ball gown.'

Emma traced the leaf-like pattern of the lace.

'Wow… You're amazing. So talented. So smart and beautiful. So everything.'

So single, Jaz thought with a sharp pang. 'Hey, do you fancy a part-time job after school or at weekends? I could do with a little help and I can give you some tips on pattern-making and stuff.'

Emma's face brightened as if someone had turned a bright light on inside her. 'Do you mean it? *Really?*'

'Sure,' Jaz said. 'Who wants to work for a fast-food chain when you can work for one of London's up-and-coming bridal designers?'

Take that, Imposter Syndrome.

Three weeks later…

'Jake, can I get you another beer?' Flynn Carlyon asked on his way to the bar at Julius's stag night. 'Hey, you haven't finished that one—you've barely taken a mouthful. You not feeling well or something?'

Jake forced a quick smile. 'No, I'm good.'

He wasn't good. He was sick. Not physically but emotionally. He hadn't eaten a proper meal in days. He couldn't remember the last time he'd had a decent sleep. Well, he could, but remembering the last time he'd made love with Jaz caused him even more emotional distress.

Yes, *emotional* distress.

The dreaded E-word—the word he'd been trying to escape from for the last few weeks. Maybe he'd been trying to escape it for the last seven years. He couldn't stop thinking about Jaz. He couldn't get the taste of her out of his mouth. He couldn't get the feel of her out of his body. It had been nothing short of torture to drop in the business plan for her last week and not touch her. She had seemed a little distracted, but when she told him she'd employed Emma Madden to help in the shop after school he'd put it down to that—Jaz was worried he would have a problem with it. He didn't. He thought it was a stroke of genius, actually. He wished he'd thought of it himself.

Julius came over with a basket of crisps. 'He's off his food, his drink and his game,' he said to Flynn. 'He hasn't looked twice at any of the waitresses, even the blonde one with the big boobs.'

Flynn grinned. 'No kidding?'

'I reckon it's because he's in love with Jaz,' Julius said. 'But he's too stubborn to admit it.'

Jake glowered at his twin. 'Just because you're getting married tomorrow doesn't mean everyone else wants to do the same.'

'Mum's still not speaking to him,' Julius said to Flynn. 'She quite fancied having Jaz as a daughter-in-law.'

'Pity she isn't so keen on having Kat Winwood as a daughter,' Flynn said wryly.

'So, how's all that going with you and Kat?' Jake said, desperate for a subject change. 'You convinced her to come to Dad's Sixty Years in Showbiz party yet?'

'Not so far but I'm working on it,' Flynn said with an enigmatic smile.

'Better get your skates on, mate,' Julius said. 'You've only got a month and a bit. The party's in January.'

'Leave Kat Winwood to me,' Flynn said. 'I know how to handle a feisty Scotswoman.'

'I bet you've handled a few in your time,' Jake said.

'You can talk,' Flynn said with another grin. 'How come you haven't handled anyone since Jaz?'

Good question. Why hadn't he? Because he couldn't bear to wipe out the memory of her touch with someone else. He didn't want anyone else. But Jaz wanted marriage and kids. He had never seen himself as a dad. He had always found it so…terrifying to be responsible for someone else. He was better off alone. Single and loving it, that was his credo.

Jake put his untouched beer bottle down. 'Excuse me,' he said. 'I'm going to have an early night. See you lot in church.'

'You look amazing, Holly,' Jaz said outside the church just before they were to enter for Julius and Holly's wedding. 'Doesn't she, Miranda?'

Miranda was wiping at her eyes with a tissue. 'Capital A amazing. Gosh, I've got to get control of myself. My make-up is running. If I'm like this as a bridesmaid, what I am going to be like as a bride?'

Holly smiled at both of them. She was a radiant bride, no two ways about that. But happiness did that to you, Jaz thought. There could be no happier couple than Julius and Holly... Well, there was Miranda and Leandro, who were also nauseatingly happy. It was downright painful to be surrounded by so many blissfully happy people.

But Jaz was resolved. She wasn't settling for anything but the real deal. Love without limits.

That was what she wanted. Love that would last a lifetime.

Love that was authentic and real, not pretend.

As Jaz led the way down the aisle she saw Jake standing next to Julius. It was surreal to see them both dressed in tuxedos looking exactly the same. No one could tell them apart, except for the way Julius was looking at Holly coming behind Miranda. Had a man ever looked at a woman with such love? *Yes*, Jaz thought when she caught a glimpse of Leandro, who was standing next to Jake looking at Miranda as if she was the most adorable girl in the world. Which she was, but that was beside the point. It was so *hard* not to be jealous.

Why couldn't Jake look at her like that?

Jaz caught his eye. He was looking a little green about the gills. Her own stomach lurched. Her heart contracted. Had he hooked up with someone last night after Julius's stag night? Had he had a one-nighter with someone? Several someones? She hadn't heard anything much in the press about him since they had announced they'd ended their 'engagement'. But then she had been far too busy with getting Holly's dress done on time to be reading gossip columns.

Miranda had let slip that Jake had left the stag night early. Did that mean he had hooked up with someone? One of the barmaids at the wine bar the boys had gone to? Why else would he leave early? He was the party boy who was usually the last man standing. It didn't bear thinking about. It would only make the knot of jealousy tighten even more in the pit of her stomach. She had to put a brave face on. She couldn't let her feelings about Jake interfere with Julius and Holly's big day.

Jaz smiled at Elisabetta and Richard Ravensdale, who were sitting together and giving every appearance of being a solid couple, but that just showed what excellent actors they both were. Elisabetta had dressed the part, as she always did. She would have outshone the bride but Jaz had made sure Holly's dress was a show-stopper. Holly looked like a fairy-tale princess. Which was how it should be, as she'd had a pretty ghastly life up until she'd met Julius, which kind of made Jaz feel hopeful that dreams did come true…at least sometimes.

The service began and Jaz tried not to look at Jake too much. She didn't want people speculating or commenting on her single status. Or worse—pitying her. Would she ever be seen as anything other than the charity case? The gardener's daughter who'd made good only by the wonderful largesse of the Ravensdales?

Even the business plan Jake had drawn up for her was another example of how much she owed them. He wouldn't take a penny for his time. He hadn't stayed for a coffee or anything once he'd talked her through the plan. He hadn't even kissed her on the cheek or touched her in any way.

But looking at him now brought it all back. How much she missed him. How much she loved him. Why couldn't he love her?

Young Emma was right—they were perfect together. Jake made her feel safe. He watched out for her the way she longed for a partner to do. He stood up *to* her and stood up *for* her. How could she settle for anyone else? She would never be happy with anyone else. It wouldn't matter how many times she got engaged, no one would ever replace Jake. Nor would she want them to.

Jake was her soul mate because only with him could she truly be herself.

The vows were exchanged and for the first time in her life Jaz saw Julius blinking away tears. He was always so strong, steady and in charge of his emotions. He was the dependable twin. The one everyone went to when things were dire. Seeing him so happy made her chest feel tight. She wanted that same happiness for herself. She wanted it so badly it took her breath away to see others experiencing it.

Jake was still looking a little worse for wear. What was *wrong* with him? Didn't he have the decency to pull himself together for his brother's wedding? Or maybe it was the actual wedding that was making him look so white and pinched. He hated commitment. It had been bad enough at the wedding expo, although she had to admit he'd put on a good front. Maybe some of that Ravensdale acting talent had turned up in his genes after all. He could certainly do with some of it now. The very least he could do was look happy for his twin brother. He fumbled over handing Julius the wedding rings. He had to search in his pocket three times. But at least he had remembered to bring them.

Jaz decided to have a word with him while they were out with the bride and groom for the signing of the register. If she could put on a brave front, then so could he. He would spoil the wedding photos if he didn't get his act together. She wasn't going to let anyone ruin Julius and Holly's big day. No way.

Jake couldn't take his eyes off Jaz. She looked amazing in her bridesmaid dress. It was robin's-egg blue and the colour made her eyes pop and her creamy skin glow. How he wanted to touch that skin, to feel it against his own. His fingers ached; his whole body ached to pull her into his arms and kiss her, to show her how much he missed her. Missed what they'd had together.

Seeing his identical twin standing at the altar as his bride came towards him made Jake feel like he was seeing another version of himself. It was like seeing what he might have been. What he could *have* if he were a better man. A more settled man—a man who could be relied on; a man who could love, not just physically, but emotionally. A man who could commit to a woman because he could see no future without her by his side. A man who could be mature enough to raise a family and support them and his wife through everything that life threw at them.

That was the sort of man his twin was.

Why wasn't *he* like that?

Or was he like that in the part of his soul he didn't let anyone see? Apart from Jaz, of course. She had seen it. And commented on it.

Jake gave himself a mental shake. No wonder he hated weddings. They made him antsy. Restless.

Frightened.

For once he didn't shove the thought back where it came from. It wasn't going back in any case. It was front and centre in his brain. He *was* frightened. Frightened he wouldn't be good enough. Frightened he would love and not be loved in return. Frightened of feeling so deeply for someone, allowing someone to have control over him, of making himself vulnerable in case they took it upon themselves to leave.

He loved Jaz.

Hadn't he always loved her? Firstly as a surrogate sister and then, when she'd morphed into the gorgeous teenager with those bedroom eyes, he had been knocked sideways. But she had been too young and he hadn't been ready to admit he needed someone the way he needed her.

But he was an adult now. He'd had a taste of what they could be together—a solid team who complemented each other perfectly. She was his equal. He admired her tenacity, her drive, her passion, her talent. She was everything he wanted in a partner.

Wasn't that why he'd been carrying the engagement ring she had given back to him everywhere he went? It was like a talisman. The ring of truth. He loved Jaz and always would.

How could he have thought he could be happy without her? He had been nothing short of morose since they'd ended their fling. He was the physical embodiment of a wet weekend: gloomy, miserable, boring as hell. He had been dragging himself through each day. He hadn't dated. He hadn't even looked at anyone. He couldn't bear the thought of going through the old routine of chatting some woman up only so he could have sex with her. He was tired of no-strings sex. No-strings sex was boring. He wanted emotional sex, the sort of sex that spoke to his soul, the kind of sex that made him feel alive and fulfilled as a man.

He had to talk to Jaz. He had to get her alone. How long was this wretched service going to take? Oh, they were going to sign the wedding register. Great. He might be able to nudge Jaz to one side so he could tell her the words he had told no one before.

Jaz wasted no time in sidling up to Jake when Julius and Holly were occupied with signing the register. 'What is *wrong* with you?' she said in an undertone.

'I have to talk to you,' he said, pulling at his bow tie as if it were choking him.

She rolled her eyes. 'Look, I know this is torture for you, but can you just allow your brother his big day without drawing attention to yourself? It's just a bow tie, for pity's sake.'

He took her by the hand, his eyes looking suspiciously moist. Did he have an allergy? There were certainly a lot of flowers about. But then the service had been pretty emotional. Maybe it was a twin thing. If Julius cried, Jake would too, although she had never seen it before.

'I love you,' he said.

Jaz's eyelashes flickered at him in shock. *'What?'*

His midnight-blue eyes looked so amazingly soft she had to remind herself it was actually Jake looking at her, not Julius looking at Holly. 'Not just as a friend,' he said. 'And not just as a lover, but as a life partner. Marry me, Jaz. Please?'

Jaz's heart bumped against her breastbone. 'You can't ask me to marry you in the middle of your brother's wedding!'

He grinned. 'I just did. What do you say?'

She gazed at him, wondering if wedding fever had got to her so bad she was hallucinating. Was he really telling her he loved her and wanted to marry her? Was he really looking at her as if she was the only woman in the world who could ever make him completely happy? 'You're not doing this as some sort of joke, are you?' she asked, narrowing her eyes in suspicion. It would be just like him to want to have a laugh to counter all the emotion, to tone down all the serious-ness, responsibility and formality.

He gripped her by the hands, almost crushing her bridesmaid's bouquet in the process. 'It's no joke,' he said. 'I love you and want to spend the rest of my life proving it to you. The last three weeks have been awful without you. You're all I think about. I'm like a lovesick teenager. I can't get you out of my head. As soon as I saw you walking down the aisle, I realised I couldn't let another day—another minute—go by without telling you how I feel. I want to be with you. Only you. Marry me, my darling girl.'

Jaz was still not sure she could believe what she was hearing. And nor, apparently, could the bridal party as they had stalled in the process of signing the register to watch on with beaming faces. 'But what about kids?' she said.

'I love kids. I'm a big kid myself. Remember how great I was with you and Miranda when you were kids? I reckon I'll be a great dad. How many do you want?'

Jaz remembered all too well. He had been fantastic with her and Miranda, making them laugh until their sides had ached. It was her dream coming to life in front of her eyes. Jake wanted to marry her and he wanted to have babies with her. 'Two at least,' she said.

He pulled her closer, smiling at her with twinkling eyes. 'I should warn you that twins run in my family.'

Jaz smiled back. 'I'll take the risk.'

'So you'll marry me?'

Could a heart burst with happiness? Jaz wondered. It certainly felt like hers was going to. But, even better, it looked like Jake was feeling exactly the same way. 'Yes.'

Jake bent his head to kiss her mouth with such heart-warming tenderness it made Jaz's eyes tear up. When he finally lifted his head, she saw similar moisture in his eyes. 'I was making myself sick with worry you might say no,' he said.

She stroked his jaw with a gentle hand, her heart now feeling so full it was making it hard for her to breathe. 'You're not an easy person to say no to.'

He brushed her cheek with his fingers as if to

test she was real and not a figment of his imag-ination. 'How quickly can you whip up a wed-ding dress?'

She looked at him in delighted surprise. 'You want to get married sooner rather than later?'

He pressed a kiss to her forehead, each of her eyelids, both of her cheeks and the tip of her nose. 'Yes,' he said. 'As soon as it can be ar-ranged. I don't even mind if it's in church or a garden, on the top of Big Ben or twenty leagues under the sea. I won't be happy until I can of-ficially call you my wife.'

'Ahem.' Julius spoke from behind them. 'We're the ones trying to get married here.'

Jake turned to grin at his brother. 'We should've made it a double wedding.'

Julius smiled from ear to ear. 'Congratula-tions to both of you. Nothing could have made my and Holly's day more special than this.'

Miranda was dabbing at her eyes as she came rushing over to give Jaz a bone- and bouquet-crushing hug. 'I'm so happy for you. We're finally going to be sisters. Yay!'

Jaz blinked back tears as she saw Leandro looking at Miranda just the way Jake was looking at her—with love that knew no bounds. With love that would last a lifetime.

She turned back to Jake. 'Do you still have that engagement ring?'

Jake reached into his inside jacket pocket, his eyes gleaming. 'I almost gave it to Julius instead of the wedding rings.' He took it out and slipped it on her finger. 'There. That's got to stay there now. No taking it off. Ever. Understood?'

Jaz wrapped her arms around his waist and smiled up at him in blissful joy. 'I'm going to keep it on for ever.'

* * * * *

Look out for the dramatic conclusion of
THE RAVENSDALE SCANDALS
THE MOST SCANDALOUS RAVENSDALE
Available September 2016

And if you missed where it all started,
check out
RAVENSDALE'S DEFIANT CAPTIVE
AWAKENING THE RAVENSDALE HEIRESS
Available now!